IT BEGINS . . .

Shane was reaching out to knock on the doors when they heard the sounds from inside the building, deep rhythmic, resonating booms that thundered closer. The doors slammed open with enough force to shatter the glass panes and knock him back onto the sidewalk.

At first all Aimee could see was the dark shape. She looked up as it pushed through the entranceway of the library. Her eyes tracked a boot and a leg, then the body of a man in ancient, dusty clothing. Then she saw the man's arm and what he held in his grasp as it swayed back and forth.

The rider dropped its grisly prize. It struck the earth next to the concrete path with a wet thump.

Aimee looked at the bloody, severed head, its eyes wide with terror, and gasped. A terrible screeching filled the air, and she wondered numbly where it came from. She only realized the sound was coming from her own lips when she sucked in a breath and started screaming again.

THE HOLLOW

BOOK ONE: **HORSEMAN**

BOOK TWO: **DROWNED**

BOOK THREE: **MISCHIEF**

BOOK FOUR: **ENEMIES**

THE
HOLLOW

BOOK ONE:

HORSEMAN

BY
CHRISTOPHER GOLDEN
&
FORD LYTLE GILMORE

razor
bill

The Hollow 1: Horseman

RAZORBILL

Published by the Penguin Group
Penguin Young Readers Group
345 Hudson Street, New York, New York 10014, U.S.A.
Penguin Group (USA) Inc., 375 Hudson Street, New York,
New York 10014, U.S.A.
Penguin Books Canada Ltd, 10 Alcorn Avenue, Toronto,
Ontario, Canada M4V 3B2 (a division of Pearson Penguin Canada, Inc.)
Penguin Books Ltd, 80 Strand, London WC2R 0RL, England
Penguin Ireland, 25 St Stephen's Green, Dublin 2, Ireland
(a division of Penguin Books Ltd)
Penguin Group (Australia), 250 Camberwell Road, Camberwell,
Victoria 3124, Australia (a division of Pearson Australia Group Pty Ltd)
Penguin Books India Pvt Ltd, 11 Community Centre, Panchsheel Park,
New Delhi – 110 017, India
Penguin Group (NZ), Cnr Airborne and Rosedale Roads, Albany,
Auckland 1310, New Zealand (a division of Pearson New Zealand Ltd)
Penguin Books (South Africa) (Pty) Ltd, 24 Sturdee Avenue,
Rosebank, Johannesburg 2196, South Africa

Penguin Books Ltd, Registered Offices: 80 Strand,
London WC2R 0RL, England

10 9 8 7 6 5 4 3 2 1

Interior design by Christopher Grassi

Library of Congress Cataloging-in-Publication Data

Golden, Christopher.
  Horseman / by Christopher Golden & Ford Lytle Gilmore.
    p. cm. — (The Hollow ; bk. 1)
  Summary: When a string of grisly decapitation murders occurs in the famed
village of Sleepy Hollow, newcomers Aimee and Shane Lancaster suspect a
supernatural killer.
  ISBN 1-59514-024-7 (pbk.)
  [1. Supernatural—Fiction. 2. Characters in literature—Fiction. 3. Brothers and
sisters—Fiction. 4. Sleepy Hollow (N.Y.)—Fiction. 5. Horror stories.] I. Gilmore,
Ford (Ford Lytle) II. Title. III. Series: Golden, Christopher. Hollow ; bk. 1.
  PZ7.G5646Ho 2005
  [Fic]—dc22

                                                    2004026074

Printed in the United States of America

Authors' Note

Local historians in various towns, most of them in Westchester County, New York, have argued for ages about what town or village was author Washington Irving's inspiration for the hamlet featured in his famous story "The Legend of Sleepy Hollow." For years, North Tarrytown, New York, stood firm in its claim as the main influence on the creation of that fictional town. In 1996, the village changed its name, officially, to Sleepy Hollow. If you visit Sleepy Hollow now, you'll see signs everywhere promoting the name and the image of the Headless Horseman, a boon to tourism. Despite the horror of the original tale, there seems something charming about the legend.

For the moment.

Meanwhile, readers who are familiar with Sleepy Hollow, New York (where Golden lived for three years in the early nineties), will notice that while some familiar landmarks are included, many liberties have been taken with the geography of the place.

We won't tell if you won't.

CHAPTER
ONE

AIMEE LANCASTER DIDN'T have a home anymore. Sure, there was going to be a new house, a new school, and a new town, but it wasn't *home*. She sat in the backseat of her father's car and gazed out the passenger side window at the darkened shops and neighborhoods they passed, lit by old-fashioned streetlights, and then uphill at the woods that loomed above the town.

"Doesn't look much like Boston," she said.

"It's nothing like Boston." Her father looked at her in the rearview mirror, an understanding smile crinkling the corners of his eyes. "But we all needed a change, Aimes. We all agreed."

Aimee gave him a nod. "Eyes on the road, Dad." She smiled, but only to let him know things were all right. It was a small lie and for a good cause.

Her brother, Shane, shot her a warning glance from the front passenger seat. Aimee ignored him. She didn't want to cause trouble, but there was no way she could pretend she wasn't going to miss home. Boston was

1

larger than life, a fast-paced urban sprawl with a colorful history, a jumping music scene, and about ten thousand good restaurants.

They were passing through a place called Tarrytown, a small town that just seemed old and faded to her, but according to her friend Stephie, who had been through Sleepy Hollow only last year, it was a metropolis compared to their new hometown. Pretty much everything she had seen of Westchester County, New York, was the same. Aimee figured she might get lucky and die of boredom before they ever got where they were going.

"Don't know if you guys noticed, but we're on Broadway," her dad said. "The same Broadway that goes down into Manhattan. You could walk all the way to Times Square from here."

"That's pretty cool. I wonder how long it would take." Shane was too interested, doing his best to make the big move as smooth as possible for their father.

"Forever. But it's pretty quick by train. I'm sure we'll see plenty of the city eventually. For now I'm just looking forward to, y'know, exploring what our new hometown has to offer." Once again he glanced at Aimee in the mirror.

"Broadway, huh?" she said, unable to muster up any real interest. "Doesn't look much like Times Square up here."

Her father blinked, his eyes flashing with something that she thought was anger, but then as he turned his attention to the road again, she saw the tiny shake of his head, and she knew that it was hurt. Disappointment. Alan Lancaster was doing his best, and it meant the world to his daughter, but sometimes Aimee just couldn't help making things worse.

She rested her head against the window and watched the road slide past. She didn't want to be here, but it helped to remind herself that this would be good for her father. He needed something different in his world now that he was alone. Aimee's breathing slowed as she lingered on that thought. Her father wasn't married anymore. Not because her mother had run off with the milkman or because he'd been sneaking kisses from his secretary on the sly. Once upon a time, she would have thought something like that was just about the worst thing that could happen.

But that was before her mother died.

Isabel Lancaster had lost her fight against cancer nine months earlier. *All the king's horses and all the king's men* . . . She had gone slowly, dying a little at a time as the medications failed to stop the cancer from growing and spreading. Losing her mom had changed the entire world for Aimee—had dulled her surroundings so that colors weren't as bright, sounds weren't as sharp. She missed her mother more than she'd ever imagined it was possible to miss anyone. And that, if nothing else, she had in common with her father and her brother.

Shane was doing his best to be excited about the

move, though Aimee knew he hadn't wanted to leave Boston any more than she had. Dad had wanted a change for himself, for all of them. When he'd run across the job listing for editor of the *Sleepy Hollow Gazette*, he'd thought it was fate. Their mother had ancestors from there, way back somewhere in the family tree. She'd also said one of her ancestors was king of Norway or something. Aimee figured they were just lucky their father hadn't found an ad for a job *there*.

Despite her doubts, Aimee did think there might be a few advantages to the move. Her dad had worked insane hours and always seemed stressed during his time at the *Boston Herald*. He hadn't been around all that much before her mother had gotten sick. It had changed him. He had seemed to age ten years in the last months of her mother's life. Aimee knew that he had wanted this move to give them all a simpler life and to focus on what really mattered, and she hoped that maybe the change would give him back that decade he had lost.

A new start would probably be good for Shane too. She loved her brother most days, but his social skills needed a total overhaul. There was nothing obviously wrong with Shane; he was just quiet. He dressed all right and wasn't bad looking, so he'd managed to avoid being labeled a total geek. But it was a near thing. Aimee figured in Sleepy Hollow he'd have the chance to reinvent himself. If he wanted to.

And she knew Sleepy Hollow could be a clean slate

for her too. Something about her seemed to rub most of her teachers the wrong way. Probably it was the need to actually state her opinions. And there was the little incident with the joyride in Mr. Garbarino's car.

Maybe it won't be so bad, she thought.

Her father glanced at her in the rearview mirror and smiled. "Almost there. Less than a mile to go."

Through the front window she could see the sign that greeted all travelers: WELCOME TO SLEEPY HOLLOW. WE'RE GLAD YOU'RE HERE. Shane looked over his shoulder at her and opened his mouth to say something just as they moved past the sign that welcomed them to their new hometown.

Before he could say a word, the car bucked violently under them and Shane's whole body lifted hard enough for him to smack the crown of his skull into the car ceiling. At almost the same instant the windshield split down the center with a loud crack, a white line fragmenting the view of the town as they entered.

"What the hell?" Her father pulled to the side of the road, clenching the wheel as the car bucked again and the engine seized. Alan managed to get the car to the curb just as it stopped rolling. His eyes were wide and he was breathing fast. All three of them looked at the broken windshield, the lightning stroke that marred the glass, in utter silence, too shocked to speak for a moment.

Shane cleared his throat and rubbed the sore spot on the top of his head. "Hey, welcome to Sleepy

Hollow." His tone was light, but his voice came out a little higher than usual.

And then everything went a little crazy.

At the same time that Alan was wrestling with the station wagon, the streetlight directly in front of the car popped in a shower of glass and sparks. Almost immediately the one next in line joined in on the fun and exploded with an arc of electricity. And then the next and the next. The light that illuminated the parking lot of the convenience store went with an explosive rush of sparks and showering glass. People ran out of the store to see what was causing the chaos and noise. A few of them immediately ran back in, cursing and screaming in panic as the glass fell.

From the bank of the Hudson River all the way up the hill to the Old Dutch Church, dogs started barking wildly, some howling. All through the town animals grew alert and panicked. In the woods surrounding the area and down virtually every street, thousands of birds launched themselves into the air, including caged parrots and lovebirds that crashed against their enclosures, breaking bones and wings and drawing blood.

In the Hudson the waters seethed, disturbed by waves of pressure that rose from below and sent shock waves and splashes all along the shore. If someone had looked just the right way, they'd have seen how the very

6

water itself took form and reached toward the shore with grasping hands.

At the Van Brunt family house four very well trained hunting dogs cut loose with a series of howls that sent chills down Derek Van Brunt's shoulders and neck. Out in the yard his father told the animals to shut up, an angry edge in his voice. Derek listened and realized it was more than just his father's hunting dogs—there were howls coming from just about everywhere.

He looked out the window at his father's broad-shouldered silhouette and saw the hounds beyond him. The dogs were completely ignoring his father's wrath, all of them tense and trembling as they cried and moaned for no reason.

In his room, Mark Hyde set down his free weights and looked over at his hamster, Robert Louis, with concern. The animal was terrified, slamming himself into the walls of the cage as he ran in circles trying to escape something only he could see. Mark moved to the cage and looked down, horrified, as the hamster capsized his food bowl and hit the water bottle on the side of the cage hard enough to knock it free.

Worry overrode common sense and Mark reached into the cage, trying to stop the rodent before he could do himself any real damage. He was too late. Robert Louis was already bleeding. As Mark reached in to capture him, the hamster crawled feebly into the corner of the cage closest to the bedroom door and shivered. Mark petted the hamster softly, frowning, as Robert Louis let out small, terrified squeaks and did his best to get away from the open window.

Mark looked at it for a few seconds, frowning. R. L. Stevenson, the hamster, normally loved to walk the edge of the window, sometimes even pressing his face against the open screen and exploring the world beyond the bedroom. Whatever was going through his mind had changed that.

On Federal Avenue, not far at all from Broadway, in a house that had been around since Sleepy Hollow was first settled, Stasia Traeger sat in her room, reading. On a normal night Stasia's room was her escape from everything that was going wrong, but just at the moment that wasn't working the way it was supposed to. The night was fairly warm and she had settled herself on the bed with the stereo playing exactly the sort of music she knew drove her mom crazy while she read a book that she knew would put her father on edge. It wasn't that she didn't love her parents or that she really felt the need to antagonize them; she just made her own choices. Her parents were both down at the restaurant anyway. But then, they were almost always at the restaurant.

Stasia set down her book and stretched, then quickly covered herself with her arms as an icy chill descended upon the room. Dressed only in jogging shorts and a T-shirt, she shivered. The cold seemed to be sweeping in from the hallway. She rubbed her hands over her arms for warmth and reached for her comforter.

Suddenly she saw something move in the hallway outside her door. Her pulse quickened. She only caught it from the corner of her eye, and when she turned to look full-on, there was nothing to see. Her breath fogged in the air.

The window was closed and the air-conditioning was off. The only breeze came from the ceiling fan whispering softly above her bed. Yet with each exhalation her breath was visible. Stasia scooted to the top of her bed where it was edged into the corner of the room and looked around, sure that somehow someone was playing with her. She had her little reputation at school and she knew a few kids who wouldn't be above pulling a stunt or two. But there was no one. She was sure of it.

Until she heard the creaking of heavy steps on the hardwood floor just outside her bedroom. Stasia shivered in wide-eyed silence as the sounds came closer and then gradually moved away. Gooseflesh rose on her skin. The sound of the bedroom window creaking made her turn her head. In that instant it happened again. From the corner of her eye she saw a figure pass her open door, but when she looked, there was no one in the hallway. She pushed her back tighter against the wall, pulling her legs up beneath her, heart pounding. Her throat was dry and she licked her lips. She didn't want to take her eyes off the bedroom door, but there had been something wrong with her window. At last she glanced over at it again. The glass was coated in frost.

For two minutes she remained completely still, only the thumping of her heart to break the silence. By then the cold had faded away. The rime of ice on the window took a little longer. There was no more movement in her hallway, no more noise from the window or the doorway.

She had heard stories about her house while growing up. Her father had told them to her when she was still little enough to sit on his knee. Now, watching the frost melt away, Stasia wondered if the stories were true.

The town hall was empty except for the custodian, Albert Finch, who kept the floors clean enough to eat off of, not that he'd have recommended it. Albert had finished with the floors and was working his way down the hall with a bottle of glass cleaner and a handful of paper towels when a pay phone started ringing. The sound was enough to make him gasp in the broken silence, but it was nothing compared to the noise when every phone in the building went off at the same time. There was a cell phone in the mayor's office that the man almost never remembered, there were fourteen pay phones and more phones on desks than he could count, and they were all going off at the same time, ringing in perfect synchronization. Albert knew next to nothing about phones, but he figured that was just about impossible. The noise was immense, almost a physical wall of sound that wanted to crush him. Albert took the hint and very calmly set his supplies on his cart before he ran from the building. For all he knew it was a terrorist. For all he knew it was a ghost. Either way, he wasn't taking any chances.

In the Old Dutch Settlers Cemetery, certainly the oldest cemetery in Sleepy Hollow, the wind tore across the trees with a savagery normally left for hurricanes and scattered the occasional shred of trash or gathering of leaves. The air danced with the litter of man and nature alike in a freakish ballet of winds that screamed and howled above the headstones. Below the strange tempest the ground trembled for a second, and then, with a sound like gunshots in a cavern, seven headstones at the very center of the cemetery cracked in half. The fine dust of broken granite and marble fell to the ground around the ruined markers, not touched at all by the howling maelstrom above. A moment later the storm simply stopped, and the leaves and discarded paper cups and newspapers that had made their home in the old cemetery fell to the ground. Seven gravestones lay where they had fallen.

At St. Michael's Catholic Church the Saturday night services were just ending. The few parishioners in attendance rose from their seats and nodded quietly to one another or to Father Patrick. The air was oppressive within those walls. Most of the faithful left quickly, and even Father Patrick made his way back to the rectory in haste. In their wake the church was silent, except for a faint hissing noise. In the small bowls fixed to the walls on either side of each entryway holy water boiled and clouds of steam rose and drifted across the room with a horrible stench.

Shane got out of the car and stared up Broadway. Up the road he saw another streetlight blink out. *Freaky.* His father climbed from the station wagon, scowling. All three of them had sat still for a moment, shaken by the sudden fits the car had decided to throw and by the sound of the windshield cracking. In the distance they could hear dogs howling and what sounded like cats in a death match, screeching at one another.

"That's a hell of a stunt," their father said, shaking his head and slapping a hand down on the roof of the car. "Punks."

"Huh?" Aimee was her normal eloquent self.

Shane looked at his father. "You think someone did this to the car?"

His dad gestured to the windshield and then to the broken light above them. "The windshield didn't crack itself, and I can't imagine the light up there was just in the mood to break either."

Shane looked around in the near darkness and

nodded. "Yeah, but Dad, *all* the streetlights are broken. And what about the car stalling?"

Alan sighed. "The car's been overheating for a while. As for the lights, power surges happen. Any way you look at it, some idiots are playing dangerous games. If the windshield had shattered instead of cracked, somebody could have been killed."

Shane furrowed his brow, still feeling like something weirder than a plain old prank had just happened.

Aimee scuffed at something on the ground near her foot. "Can we just go? I want to get unpacked tonight."

"Yeah, honey. We can." Alan scanned the area, his face unreadable. "Still, I've got to say they have strange ways of welcoming people around here."

The three of them climbed back into the car and headed north toward their new home.

CHAPTER
TWO

THEIR FATHER HAD been to Sleepy Hollow before, but Aimee and Shane had only seen photographs of their new house. The pictures hadn't done it justice—it was much bigger than they'd expected. Aimee walked around, slack jawed, her eyes drinking in every detail of the old colonial. Ten rooms on two floors, plus a full attic and basement.

"Okay, Shane. Dibs," Aimee said as soon as she spotted the first bedroom upstairs, a medium-size room with a little alcove by the window.

"I don't think so. As firstborn I get to decide."

"Get a clue. I saw it first—it's mine."

Alan gave them a quick eye roll before he moved into the room he had already claimed as his home office.

They finally settled the bedroom debate once Shane decided he liked the view better from the other bedroom anyway. But it was only a couple of minutes before they were at it again, this time over who got to use what part of the storage space in their shared bathroom.

Once everything had been settled, Aimee sank down onto the sofa in the living room. She couldn't help feeling like she'd forgotten something important, but she realized it was just the sensation she was getting from being in the wrong place with the right furniture. Everything was theirs, but it would take a while for her to adjust to seeing it all in different locations than where it had been back in Boston.

"Isabel would have loved this place." Her dad sat down near her, his arm sliding around her shoulders.

"You done good, Pa." She threw a little extra twang into the words. Her dad had promised her that Sleepy Hollow wasn't really in the sticks, and ever since, she'd ragged him with a thick country accent. He smiled and kissed the top of her head.

"So, what's your brother doing up there?"

Aimee groaned. "Unloading his books. I swear he should just open his own used bookstore."

"Nothing wrong with liking books."

"Even when he likes them more than people?"

"Shane's just more cautious than you are, honey. He has an old soul."

"Dad, there's old and then there's mummified."

Her father shook his head. "Not everyone can be quite as . . . uninhibited as you."

"What do you mean by that?" She leaned away from him, feeling a twinge of hurt.

"Shane just tends to think before he reacts. He likes

15

a road map and you just like to follow the road and see where it goes." He stood and shoved his hands into his pockets. "I'm not saying either one is right or wrong; I'm just saying you two have different ways of doing things."

"Well, his is boring."

Alan laughed. "That's my girl," he said, relaxing for the first time since they'd arrived.

The next morning started off with breakfast at the Muffin Man, a small restaurant with a big menu. Shane ate like a pig, his appetite on a rampage. Aimee did a pretty good job of keeping up with him, and even their dad managed to kill off most of the massive portion of eggs and sausage on his breakfast plate. The food was fantastic.

They'd left the car at home and walked to the diner, and afterward they headed over to the offices of the *Sleepy Hollow Gazette*. Alan wasn't really supposed to start his job as editor in chief until Monday, but the owner had asked him to stop by for a quick meeting, even though it was a Sunday. Shane hoped that wasn't a sign of things to come.

The office was about what Shane expected: small and cluttered. Their father was apparently the only full-time employee. There were a couple of freelance photographers, an old woman who was a part-time receptionist, several writers who contributed from time to time, and Professor Bisby, a drama professor at Marymount College down in Tarrytown, who wrote about the local arts scene. Bisby looked like he probably slept in a plastic bubble to avoid any sort of dirt. His hair was slicked back with enough goo to grease down a dozen scalps and his tweed jacket was perfectly creased. With his bow tie to top off the look, he seemed like he had stepped out of another time and had no idea that the world around him was any different from the one he came from. Introductions were made all around, but the only name that stuck for Shane was Bisby's.

None of them were going to be stalking the darker, seamier parts of Sleepy Hollow in pursuit of a Pulitzer Prize, and Shane had to wonder if his father was already regretting the decision to move to the small town.

Aimee glanced around the small office with a look on her face that would have worked just as well if she'd swallowed a bug. Alan was talking to the staff, and they all listened, rapt. He was a big-city editor, after all. Sleepy Hollow wasn't some hick town—not this close to Manhattan—but the newspaper mostly carried wire reports. From what Shane's dad had said, its local news consisted of a crime beat, articles scattered here and there, and wedding announcements and obituaries.

When the phone rang, his father looked directly at Shane and gestured for him to answer it. He nodded and picked up the receiver. "*Sleepy Hollow Gazette,* can I help you?"

Before the person on the other end could even speak, the phone rang again and Shane nudged his sister. She sighed dramatically and reached for the phone on her father's desk.

Shane turned his attention back to his caller. The guy's voice was deep and nasal. "Yeah, look, I just wanted to let someone over there know that something really strange is going on in town."

"Strange how?"

"Well, for starters, someone broke every streetlight on my whole street last night."

Shane wondered how close the guy lived to Broadway. Maybe the weird light thing had happened on more than one street. He grabbed a pen and pad of paper, ready to take down any additional info.

"I know what you're going to say," the caller continued, "'cause my wife said the same thing. Some kind of short circuit or something, right? So how do you explain Hizzoner?"

Shane blinked. *His Honor?* he wondered, confused. "Like . . . a judge?"

"No, Hizzoner the dog!"

"There's a dog called Hizzoner?"

"Yeah, where've you been all your life?"

"Boston."

"Oh. Anyways, I'm coming back from the grocery store and damn near ran Hizzoner over. Biggest dog anyone ever saw. Started chasing me. I hit the gas and I swear I was doing forty before I lost it. Never seen anything like it. Huge! Black. And it had these eyes, like it had a fire in its skull that wanted out. I mean the thing was breathing fire at me!"

"And did you call the police, sir?"

"They didn't want to listen. The cops in this town never listen to anything you have to say. They disgust me! When the UFOs were buzzing my house and them little green men were running all over my backyard and I called the police, do you think they showed up? No. No, they did not! Let my stupid neighbor with her damned cats get a kitten in a tree and the fire department, the cops, and the local VFW all show up to save the damned day. But if I have a problem with things running around in the woods and glowing lights hanging around my back porch, all I get is, 'We'll be there as soon as we can,' and they never show up! That's the problem with Sleepy Hollow! There's no one you can call with a real problem around here!"

Shane grinned. The guy was a serious nutcase. Still, he wrote down every detail anyway, remembering what his father had told him were the most important parts of any story: who, what, when, where, how, and why. Apparently there was a really big dog out near the intersection of Waldsburg Street and Beakman. Shane thought of all of the howling the night before, the dogs going crazy, and gave the guy's story a little more credence despite the fact that he sounded like a loon overall.

"You have an obligation to tell people about that dog and I'm not kidding," the man was saying. "I've got the marks on my car's rear bumper as evidence."

"Sir, I promise you I'll pass the information on to the editor. Can I get your name, address, and phone number so he can have a reporter get back in touch with you if he needs to?"

The man obliged and Shane wrote it down, resisting the urge to draw in a few doodles of a man in a straitjacket in the process. Still, if Mr. Wack Job claimed he had evidence on his car, then obviously *something* had happened.

Shane hung up the phone and sighed, just in time to have the line ring again. This caller was a woman who sounded like she was probably somewhere in her sixties. Her story was a little different but just as bizarre—something about a man on horseback trampling through her front yard and tearing up her rosebushes. Shane promised to pass the information on again and jotted down the address.

After five calls for him and around as many for Aimee, the staff meeting was over. Shane gathered up his notes and put them in order. Two more people had called about the black dog, and another claimed there was someone whispering obscenities out in the woods behind her house. He'd stopped wanting to sneer by the time they were done. Every last one of the callers sounded genuinely worried or even angry about the disturbances. It was hard to imagine that they were all just calling in with jokes or all delusional.

The next time the phone rang, Professor Bisby nodded to him and took it, smiling a dismissal in his direction. "Goodness, I have no idea what's gotten into people. I don't usually get this many calls in a day."

"Okay, well, that's one lunatic and a lot of strange sightings." Shane looked at Aimee as he gathered his collection of notes to give his father.

"What do you mean?"

"The first guy was going off about a giant dog, and the weird thing is, I actually had other calls about that, but that guy also thinks there're aliens sneaking into his backyard and bugging his house."

"That doesn't mean he's a lunatic, Shane." Aimee wiggled her eyebrows. "Open your mind to the possibilities," she teased.

Their father walked over to join them and Aimee handed him the stack of messages she'd written down. "Looks like you were busy, honey. Anything worth noticing?" he asked.

"Yeah, Dad. According to Shane, you have a lot of weirdos in Sleepy Hollow."

Alan grinned and raised one eyebrow like he was waiting for the punch line to a joke he knew would be bad. "What do you mean?"

She ticked off the cases on her fingers. "Two people called about a black dog the size of a motorcycle, one guy said the walls in his house bled last night, a lady swears her lawn tried to attack her, and a kid says it was raining frogs at his house. And Shane has even more for you."

Shane took his cue and handed his dad a stack of notes. "She's right. Freaks-and-geeks time in Sleepy Hollow. If it's like this all the time, you should work for the *National Enquirer* instead."

Alan looked at him and wagged a finger good-naturedly. "Wash your mouth out." He turned to Aimee. "You know, it's probably just a bunch of your future classmates doing a prank phone call marathon. Or maybe that electrical surge last night just got people's imaginations working overtime."

The door to the *Gazette* offices opened and a policeman entered. Shane looked him over, feeling his body stiffen. Even though he hadn't done anything wrong, he couldn't help being hyper-aware that the cop's presence meant potential trouble. *Authority as a source of fear,* he mused. *Maybe I've got a guilty conscience.*

Since the staff meeting was officially over, everyone but Professor Bisby filed out of the office, some nodding to the cop as they moved toward the doors. Bisby stayed behind, sitting at a desk and jotting notes as the Lancasters studied the policeman.

He was a big man but not fat. He was maybe six feet tall and either worked out regularly or was just one of those men designed to look like he pumped iron. His hair was black and his eyes were a kind of snowy-day gray Shane had never seen before.

The man stepped forward and extended his hand to Shane's father. "Mr. Lancaster? I'm Ed Burroughs, the chief of police here in Sleepy Hollow."

"Nice to meet you, Ed. Call me Alan." Mr. Lancaster shook the officer's hand firmly.

Burroughs looked around the office, nodding to Shane and Aimee and smiling at the professor. "Mike," he said. Bisby nodded back and answered the phone again.

"Looks like last night is already keeping you busy," the chief said. "That's why I figured I'd stop by and give you a visit. A lot of people prefer to call the newspaper instead of calling the police. I thought you might have heard a thing or two that I hadn't."

"Mostly a number of people who were upset about the streetlights all being blown out," Alan replied. "Mike received a few calls earlier about some vandalism at an old cemetery here in town, and apparently two or three people have called in about a big black dog terrorizing them."

"Hizzoner." The chief sighed, exasperated.

"Excuse me?"

Chief Burroughs gave them a weary smile. "There's a legend around here. People grow up hearing stories from their grandparents, so they see some big stray in a field or something and get spooked. Every once in a while some yahoo calls in to complain about a big black dog."

"So you don't think there's any danger of a wild dog

23

coming into the area or anything?" Shane had opened his mouth before he even realized that he was going to. "Because the man I was talking to on the phone swears it came after him in his car and did some damage to the rear fender."

Chief Burroughs looked at him and nodded. "See? Hey, you never know. I'll certainly be on the lookout for a giant feral dog, but you can mark my words, we'll get a dozen or more claims that there's a big black dog with fiery red eyes and teeth as big as steak knives before it's all said and done."

"Just the same, I think I should warn people to be careful, especially with the streets blacked out," Alan said. "I'll make a note to add that to the Around Town column."

"Yeah, what about the lights?" Aimee spoke up. "What do you think happened with those?"

"I'm guessing some kid tried tapping into the Westchester power system and sent through enough juice to blow them all out." The chief's eyebrows knitted as he spoke. "I have a few of my more computer-savvy guys trying to figure out how it was done. That was a dangerous and stupid stunt, to say nothing of what it's costing to replace that many lights. Half of the streets in town are going to be blacked out until we can get enough replacements to fix this mess."

Aimee blinked and looked at the man. "You think *kids* did this?"

Chief Burroughs crossed his arms. "It wouldn't be

the first time we had a few kids get bored and try screwing with the town by computer."

Shane frowned but kept his mouth closed. He wasn't exactly a state-of-the-art hacker or anything, but he was pretty sure there were fail-safes in the power systems of any town that would prevent that sort of power surge from happening. If there weren't all sorts of redundant protections against power surges, a single lightning strike would take out a town, to say nothing of the havoc it would cause in a place like Boston. Besides, the streetlights probably weren't linked to a source of power separate from everything else in town.

Shane tuned them all out for a minute, thinking about the first phone call he'd answered. He'd assumed pretty quickly that the guy was just crazy, but then at least five other people had called in about Hizzoner. He tried to picture a dog big enough to leave scrape marks down the back of a car and imagined what it would be like to have to run from one.

Aimee looked at her brother, then back at the building in front of them. It was a massive, sprawling thing, three stories tall and about as inviting as the average prison. More than ever, she wished she was back in Boston.

Then Shane gave her a smile and a wink that made it a little easier to look at Sleepy Hollow High and take the first step onto the premises.

Several of the locals were looking at the two of them as they moved across the courtyard toward a long stairway that led up to the school. She wanted to tell them to take a picture, it would last longer, but instead put on a bright smile that felt completely false. A few of them smiled back. Nothing special, but suddenly her own smile felt a little more genuine.

A jock with his arm around a blond girl looked their way as they approached and caught Aimee's eye for a second. She stared back, taking in his broad shoulders under the SHH letterman's jacket, his dark eyes, and his blond hair cut short, almost military style. Serious hottie. She wasn't sure, but he seemed to be checking her out. Then he looked back at the girl he was walking with, listening to something she was saying. Aimee let herself have a one-second fantasy about meeting him. Girlfriend or not, he looked like fun. Then she noticed that the couple were both looking their way—but at Shane, not at her. The girl said something else to the guy, then laughed, and suddenly his whole expression changed, his eyes hardening as he quickened his pace, leaving the girl behind.

He came up right behind Shane and Aimee. He started to walk by them, just inches away, and then shoulder-checked Shane almost hard enough to knock him on his ass. He wasn't much taller than Shane but definitely broader. Shane dropped his nearly empty book bag and the folder with copies of their school records and health forms in it and let out a small grunt of surprise. The papers scattered.

It was deliberate; there was no question. Most likely the blond chick had said something about Shane that jock boy hadn't wanted to hear.

The jock looked at Shane, his jaw muscles working overtime. "Why don't you watch where you're going?"

Aimee stepped up to the guy. "Hey! You hit *him*, loser, not the other way around."

Shane shot Aimee a warning glance and then looked at the jerk who'd bumped him. "Whatever. Sorry if I cut you off." He bent to retrieve the folder and started gathering the papers that had spilled out.

Aimee rolled her eyes. "No, Shane, he did it on purpose. I saw him. He moved over just so he could try to knock you down." She took turns glaring at her brother and at the jock. Then she looked over his shoulder to see the girl he'd been with. She was watching with raised eyebrows, as surprised as Aimee. Then she just shook her head and walked away, clearly not wanting to deal with the whole mess.

The jock looked Aimee up and down, giving his most arrogant sneer. "You need glasses."

"You need a clue."

"Hold up. You want to back off now." Shane stepped between them, facing the guy. It was okay for someone to pick on him, but Aimee knew the second anyone said anything about her, Shane would be there

27

to make them take it back. Sometimes she loved him for that and sometimes she hated him for it.

"Oh, please, you aren't really getting up in my face, are you? Seriously?" The guy loomed, puffing out his chest and glaring at Shane. He was really cute and really, really getting on Aimee's nerves. She felt her hands ball up into fists. No one got to mess with her brother but her.

Shane didn't back down, even though the guy looked like he could turn him into a pretzel. He clutched the folder in one hand, the other tightening into a fist at his side. "Look, I already apologized for what *you* did. I don't want trouble. But if you're going to talk to my sister like that, then we're going to have some." Shane's macho talk sounded entirely wrong coming from him.

Then another student shoved between Shane and the jock, breaking the moment. The kid, a short little bundle of energy, picked up Shane's book bag and shoved it at him. Shane took it with his free hand. Some of the papers were still strewn on the ground, but nobody was paying attention to them at the moment.

"Listen, guys, I'm sure that this is all a great show and that under the right circumstances, everyone here—" The newcomer paused and looked at Aimee, winking through thick glasses. "Well, maybe not you. But the rest of us would love to watch you two pummel each other. It's just a case of wrong time, wrong place."

He moved and talked so fast that Aimee could barely get a good look at him. While she was catching up to what he'd just said, she realized the guy wasn't alone. He had a friend with him. A much larger, much calmer friend, who came up behind the jock and put large hands on his shoulders. The jock turned around and went a little pale. Aimee didn't blame him. The jerk who'd shoved Shane wasn't small, but the guy standing behind him was maybe six and a half feet tall, and unlike most of the students she'd met in high school who achieved that sort of height, he wasn't at all skinny. He had a nest of brown hair that looked like it hadn't been cut in maybe six months. He also had the meanest smile she'd ever seen.

The jock looked him square in the chin and then remembered to move his eyes up to meet the gaze of the giant. "H-Hyde . . ."

"We're all friends here, Derek. Call me Mark."

"We were just—"

Mark Hyde smiled and nodded amiably, his hands still on Derek's shoulders. "We were just agreeing that this was all a mistake and leaving. Right?"

Aimee let out a breath she hadn't even realized she was holding and saw Shane do the same thing. All around them the kids who had noticed them from afar were much closer, no doubt eager for a fight that apparently wasn't going to happen.

"Yeah. Okay, Mark."

29

"Now, shake hands with our new student and introduce yourself like a human being."

Aimee looked at Mark Hyde and shook her head. He looked more like he should have been the one terrorizing the school yard instead of making everyone play nicely. There was something strange about his features—he had the kind of expression that seemed like it should qualify as ugly, just based on the fear factor of that scowl. But there was something endearing, even cute, about his face overall—something gentle behind the anger in his eyes. She hadn't believed that worked for anything but bulldogs and Chihuahuas until she saw this guy.

"That's my boy," chimed in the short guy. "Derek Van Brunt, meet . . ." He turned to Shane and pointed. "Quick, what's your name?"

"My name?" Shane looked stunned. Probably he was wondering why he hadn't had his head shattered yet. "Shane Lancaster. This is my sister—"

"Peachy." The little guy flashed a smile that made him look ten years old. "Thanks. Derek Van Brunt, meet Shane Lancaster and sis. They're new here and we want to make them feel welcome." He spoke with deliberately slow words. From the way Derek was still clenching his jaw, it looked like he probably wanted to swat the skinny kid and get back to beating up Shane, but he knew better than to piss off the short guy's giant buddy.

Derek stuck a hand out in Shane's direction and

muttered an apology he obviously didn't feel. Shane slung his book bag over his shoulder to free up his hand and shook quickly, just as obviously displeased about being there but probably at least happy to still be alive.

"Isn't it great to make new friends?" Hyde asked, obviously pleased with Van Brunt's discomfort.

Aimee was still trying to figure out the proper response when a new voice added to the mix. "Let them breathe, Mark." The voice seemed to belong to a cat, not a person. She didn't talk; she purred. "They can't be friends with your big old arms weighing them down."

For the first time since he'd shown up, the hyperactive kid in the glasses slowed down. "Oh my God! Mark! She spoke to you!"

Derek Van Brunt brushed off Mark Hyde's hand and went on his way, storming toward the school. Most of the crowd was gone, now that there seemed little chance of bloodshed, leaving Aimee staring at the only one who'd stayed behind, the source of the amazing voice—a girl who, after one glance, became Aimee's instant idol.

Everything about the girl drew your eyes right to her, from her clothes to the body under them, to the thick cascading hair, auburn with some heavy-duty red highlights, that fell around her slim, muscular shoulders. She wore black leather boots with short heels poking out from below leather pants most girls would have been terrified to be seen in. Her shirt was a standard button-up for guys, but she'd rolled up the sleeves and knotted up the bottom until it fit her properly. She had half a dozen rings on her fingers and a whole rack of multicolored bangle bracelets. Around her neck was a necklace of black onyx, complete with a Celtic cross. By Boston standards she wasn't overly extreme, but here she stood out. Her face was the sort that would make most girls hate her on general principle. She was wearing makeup but didn't need it. She had fair skin, full lips, a perfect nose with just the smallest scattering of freckles across the bridge, and a small diamond stud through the left nostril. She had wide icy blue eyes with long, thick lashes. Even her eyebrows looked perfect.

Aimee had never met a girl more obviously comfortable in her own skin, right down to the little Chinese character that was tattooed just above her pierced navel. She wasn't the only one staring, either. Every guy around her had his eyes on the girl. Even Shane was looking, and though his face remained neutral, she could just imagine the gears moving in his head.

The newcomer's lips pulled into a very small Mona Lisa smile. "Hello, Steve. Nice to see you."

The kid with the glasses looked at her and blushed slightly. He didn't say a word, just nodded.

Mark crossed his arms over his chest. Aimee noticed for the first time that he had a tattoo on his left bicep, but it was partially covered by the DISTURBED T-shirt he was wearing. Without the other two in front of him she realized again just how large he was. His heavy-metal T-shirt and jeans almost looked like a second skin—she suspected not because it was fashionable but because finding pants in his size was a bit of a challenge—and he'd finished off his clothes with a massive pair of biker's boots.

"Hi, Stasia. How's everything?" Mark spoke softly, and his eyes drank in the girl in front of him like a drowning man gulps air.

"Mark. Thanks for saving the new kids."

He shrugged and looked at her, then over at Shane. He nudged Shane with one massive paw and then waved his hand lazily in Aimee's direction. "Well, seems only fair to let them actually get into the school before they get their clothes all bloodied."

Stasia let out a small laugh that seemed to almost break the giant kid. For the first time Aimee noticed that she held a small stack of papers by her side. Now the girl glanced down at the records she'd gathered up off the ground, keeping them from scattering.

"Aimee Hastings Lancaster," she read aloud from the top paper. She glanced up, mischief in her eyes but no malice. "I'm guessing that's you." She nodded at Shane. "He doesn't look much like an Aimee."

The two girls grinned. Then Stasia glanced over at Mark and Steve. "All right, boys. Go to a class or something. I'll get these two over to the office so they can get their schedules."

Steve opened his mouth as if released from some sort of spell. "Great! That'll save me the trouble. I still have to finish my report for chemistry."

Stasia shook her head. "Isn't that due in, like, an hour?"

"Yeah, and?"

"Have you even started?"

"Of course not. What? I should do it at home?" He waved to Aimee and Shane and then started walking.

Mark nodded at the Lancasters. "Welcome to Sleepy Hollow High." Then he followed his friend.

Aimee looked at the two of them, puzzled. They had less in common than she and her brother did, and that was saying a lot as far as she was concerned.

"Hi, I'm Stasia Traeger."

Aimee turned just in time to see the girl extend a long-fingered hand to her brother, who took it and shook it as softly as if it were made of glass.

"I'm Shane and this is Aimee." He looked toward Aimee with a quick glance, then back at the girl in front of him. He smiled sheepishly and rolled his eyes. "Can you tell me what just happened?"

Stasia laughed again. "You just met Jekyll and Hyde, who were stopping Derek from breaking you into tiny pieces."

Her eyes drifted away from Shane and looked into Aimee's, and she and Aimee exchanged a smile. Aimee felt an immediate connection to Stasia, like she'd

34

entered that instant comfort zone that always happened whenever she met someone she knew could be a friend.

"I don't know if he would have broken me into—"

"Nothing personal, Shane." Stasia cut him off. "It's just what he does. Fight, I mean. I think he has a black belt or something."

Aimee looked at the dwindling figures of Jekyll and Hyde. "They're really named Jekyll and Hyde?"

"No, Steve's real last name is Delisle. The Jekyll part is just a nickname. He's kind of a nut, but also the brain of the class. They've been hanging around together for years, and since Mark's last name is Hyde, you know, the name just sort of stuck."

Stasia hooked an arm around Shane's bicep and one around Aimee's. "Let's get you enrolled. Maybe we can even get a few classes together if we work it the right way." She led and they followed. Shane kept his mouth shut and walked with a sort of stunned look on his face, though Aimee couldn't tell if it was because of what had almost happened or because a totally hot girl he barely knew was practically wrapping herself around him as they walked. She hoped it was the former. Stasia was too hot to go for quiet Shane, if she even wanted a boyfriend. Besides, Aimee was already hoping she could get to know Stasia better herself—and she wasn't about to let a crush of Shane's ruin another possible friendship before it even began.

CHAPTER
THREE

A LOT OF the day sort of blurred for Shane, which wasn't really surprising on the first day of school. He wound up in two classes with his sister, even though she was a sophomore, one year behind him. Apparently some of the classes here were mixed between grades. Which was why he *also* had those classes with Stasia, another sophomore. When she was around, he found it hard to keep his eyes off her. And when she wasn't, his mind kept going back to her.

Jekyll and Hyde were juniors like Shane, and he was psyched when he saw they had a class together, since he liked what he'd seen of them so far.

When lunchtime rolled around, Shane seated himself in a corner and pulled out his book, but he'd only read a few pages before Stasia and Aimee showed up at his table. Stasia looked at the paperback in his hand, a collection of Irish ghost stories, and arched one eyebrow but made no comment.

"So what do you guys think of all the excitement around Sleepy Hollow?" she asked instead.

"I keep hearing about this big black dog," Aimee said, leaning forward. "I mean, I just heard some kids say it chased a bunch of seniors into the woods on Saturday night. It broke up their party and almost caught one of the girls, but instead it just got her purse."

"It's not just here," Stasia said. "There are legends of black dogs all over Europe and Great Britain, but everyone in the Hollow has heard of Hizzoner. He's like a bogeyman your parents tell you about to keep you from wandering into the woods." Her voice was breathy and sultry and Shane loved it so much that he hated it.

"How do you know about black dog legends?" Shane looked at her and then back to the pseudo-lasagna on his plate.

"It's a hobby. I like reading about all that crap." She pointed to his book. "That's a good one, and I like the Haunted America series, but I think *Haunted Heartland* was better."

"I haven't read that one yet." He looked at her again, surprised to find someone else who liked to read about ghosts and other strange occurrences. *Great. She's smart, too.* He reminded himself that she wasn't exactly the sort that noticed guys like him and left it alone. "But I will."

"I'll let you borrow mine if you promise to take good care of it."

"Deal."

"Anyway," Aimee broke in. "I also heard someone

talking about a tree out in the woods that tells secrets."

"That was probably Melinda. She lives in a house that faces the woods. I heard her talking in sociology about a tree that was telling her things. She broke up with her boyfriend because he couldn't deny what the tree said."

"What did the tree say?" Shane took the bait.

Stasia's lips curved in a slight smile. "That he was getting action on the side from one of the cheerleaders."

Aimee got a scandalized grin on her face. She loved gossip, but only in small doses. Shane pushed food around on his plate. As far as he was concerned, gossip was like a bad movie without a plot. But this was a lot weirder than just some talk in the locker room. . . .

"Okay, is it just me?" he said. "Or are you two talking about a *tree* that gossips?"

"We never said it was real, Shane. It's just what people are talking about." Aimee gave him a drama queen expression and he resisted giving her the finger.

Stasia pointed to his book. "Open mind?"

He shrugged. "Skeptic. Chief Burroughs thinks it's a wild dog and kids blowing out the lights. I think something weird happened in this town, or a lot of drugs were slipped into everyone's brownies."

Stasia rolled her eyes and sipped from her milk carton. "Chief Burroughs isn't exactly open to suggestions."

"He did seem a little less than willing to stretch his imagination." Shane smiled wryly and was rewarded by a grin from Stasia.

Aimee shrugged and finished a bite of salad. "He's not paid to think. He's paid to enforce the law."

"He'd better start thinking," Stasia said. "I don't know if I want to be around Sleepy Hollow for much longer if he doesn't."

For some reason, Shane felt a chill as she said the words.

Saying that Alice Moncrief liked cats was sort of like saying that the sun could be a little bright at noon on a clear summer day. On the cats' part, the feeling was mutual. Alice had been raising cats in her old house for almost a decade. There had only been two cats when her husband, Stanley, was still alive. After he passed, she just sort of started adopting the strays that came along.

She didn't mind. She liked the extra company.

The sky outside was just fading to night and she smiled. She'd always loved twilight best of all. The cats purred and strutted as they waited for their food. Alice started opening cans and pouring another helping of dry food into the community bowl she'd long since set up in the kitchen. Jerry Springer was on TV and she listened with half an ear as another couple started squawking at each other about their infidelities. Alice would never be able to understand people. Cats, on the other hand, were predictable. Oh, they might from time to time decide that they didn't want to be petted or perhaps that they would prefer to be outside at a certain time as opposed to their usual routines, but they never disappointed her when it came to wanting their dinner.

Alice smiled, waiting for her little family to come eat. She waited for almost two minutes before she started to worry. Normally she could count on the smell of the Captain's Feast cat food to bring her babies in a hurry.

Not tonight.

For the first time in ten years, the cats didn't come. Not even when she called them all by name. Even if none of the others had shown, her pudgy Maine coon, Suzy Q, should have shown up. Suzy Q would no sooner miss a meal than she would forget to breathe. At twenty-three pounds, Suzy Q was the biggest of her cats and almost always the hungriest.

Finally Alice walked into the living room, her pulse speeding up just slightly as she wondered what she'd find.

The nerves turned to fear when she saw what was waiting for her near the television. Every one of her cats was in the room, staring at her from their perches. They were spread around the living room on the furniture, even one on top of the television set. As Alice looked at them, Suzy Q dragged one claw across the arm of her sofa and tore the fabric, spilling stuffing across the sofa and the floor beneath it.

"Suzy Q? Honey? What are you doing to Mommy's couch?" She took a step into the room and one of the tabbys brushed against the lamp on the end table near where she normally read. The lamp fell to the floor and shattered, stealing most of the light from the room.

With only the *Jerry Springer Show* to illuminate her surroundings, Alice listened to the hissing sounds coming from her cats. In the semidarkness their eyes seemed to glow and Alice looked around at the dozen pairs of green-hued pupils that stared at her, watching the tails of the cats slowly twitch from side to side.

For the first time in her life, Alice Moncrief was afraid of her pets. Before she could step from the room, the cats moved, blurring past the arguing people and the cheering audience on the screen as they came toward her on padded feet.

Alice turned and tried to run, only to have two of the cats slash savagely at her legs, drawing lines of wet fire down her calves. Another of the animals landed with frightening grace in the space between her shoulder blades and sank in with its claws, holding on as she bucked and screamed, the pain sudden and blinding.

She tried to flee into the kitchen, where the light was better, and found her feet tangled as Suzy Q ran between her ankles. She windmilled her arms in an effort to stay on her feet but failed. Alice grunted as she hit the floor and let out another cry as the cats attacked in one solid wave of fur and teeth and claws.

One of the gray, long-haired Maine coons bit down on her hand. Alice shook him, trying to knock his twisting body free, but he wrapped his forepaws around her wrist and started slashing at her arm near the elbow with savage rear claws. She let out a scream and swung

41

her arm around, slamming the cat to the floor beside her. He rolled off her, spitting and hissing.

Alice stood up again, half crushing one of her babies—her babies! How could they do this to her?—in the process. The feline let out a howl of protest and scrambled away from her. Alice ran toward the back door, hearing the hisses of the animals she loved as they charged again, slashing and biting at her and drawing blood from a dozen surprisingly deep cuts.

Suzy Q landed on Alice's head, razored claws digging into her scalp and slicing deep into her flesh, drawing blood and sending a wave of nauseating pain through her. The fat cat's claws sank in deep and slid as Alice moved, until she felt a deep flashing pain across the left side of her face and her ear. She lowered her head, nearly blind with panic, and deliberately ran herself into the wall, knocking the cat senseless. Her own vision doubled for a second, but the sharp pain of still more claws attacking quickly snapped her out of her stupor.

Alice tried for the back door. One of the kittens was climbing up the back of her thigh and biting savagely at her leg as she went. She slapped the cat away and felt another attack the offending arm. The door was locked. Alice was forced to run again, this time back into the nearly dark living room, where Jerry Springer was summing up his feelings about men who dated more than one sister at a time.

The front door was locked as well and as she tried to turn the dead bolt, one of the cats tore the skin from the back of her hand. Alice shrieked, too stunned to believe that her little ones could hurt her this way despite the wounds that bled all the evidence she could need down every limb she had and across her face.

Frantic to escape, Alice shoved her television and its stand out of her way and grabbed for the sash of the bay window. Suzy Q took a chunk of flesh out of her earlobe and tried for a second while Alice pulled at the locked frame. At last she resorted to desperate measures and balled up her fist. She punched the windowpane and it cracked in a spiderweb of fractures. She hit the weakened spot again and again until it finally shattered in a cascade of sharp fragments.

The cats yowled out their anger, hissing and spitting as they opened more wounds on her legs and back. Alice pushed herself through the opening she'd made, cutting her left palm deeply as Suzy Q ripped at her hair. She scraped the cat off against the jagged blades above her and cried out in mourning as her favorite pet fell away from her, bleeding from a gaping wound in her side.

Alice took another deep cut across her knee as she clambered through the opening. She fell from the window and landed in the shrubs growing just outside, fully expecting the cats to follow, then scrambled across the dirt and turf, panting and whining as she moved. She'd made it halfway across the lawn on her hands and knees before she realized that she was no longer being attacked.

Dazed and terrified, Alice looked back at her house and saw that none of the cats had followed. From the near-perfect darkness behind the jagged mouth broken through her bay window, she could see the cats looking at her.

None of them followed. Alice looked at the animals, a faint whimper escaping her throat as they stared back.

She sat on the lawn even after the police came, alerted by her neighbor Judith Sullivan. She sat there until the ambulance came to take her away. Alice watched the house dwindle in the rear windows of the vehicle. The cats stared back, unblinking.

CHAPTER FOUR

AIMEE ATE HER breakfast slowly, savoring every bite of the omelet her father had made. It was one of the things he always did well, and since they'd moved to Sleepy Hollow, he had a little more time in the mornings.

Of course he was on the phone already, working from home and talking to the police chief, getting answers about what had happened a couple of nights ago to an old lady in the hospital who said her cats had tried to kill her. Aimee shivered when she heard how many stitches the poor lady had. One hundred and seventeen, to be exact. When the police had tried to capture the cats to take them to a veterinarian, the cats had attacked them too. The animals had all had to be destroyed.

"Doesn't sound like a fair fight to me," Aimee said.

Shane rolled his eyes. "I don't think they went in there to kill the cats, Aimee. I think they sort of got stuck with that part."

"Cats can be fast and mean, but the cops had guns."

She picked at her breakfast. "It doesn't sound like much of a contest."

"Whatever." Shane finished inhaling his food.

Her dad set down the phone and let out a deep breath. "This town is a few apples short of a bushel."

"Is that your way of saying everyone's crazy?" Aimee asked.

"Yeah, that pretty much covers it. Someone's having a field day around here. Even in a town with so many legends this isn't normal."

Shane nodded. "More sightings of Hizzoner?"

Dad made an affirmative grunt, pouring himself another cup of coffee. "Almost every night and almost always at an intersection."

"Weird."

"It gets weirder."

"Weirder like how?" Aimee finished her breakfast. If her dad kept this up, she was going to get fat.

"Like Marybeth—the woman who does the final layouts before the paper goes to the printer every night—called the police when she pulled into her driveway last night because she was sure she'd had a break-in. She waited in her car and used the cell phone, and when the cops came, they found one of her windows open but no one in the house and nothing disturbed." He shook his head. "Or like a fisherman on the Hudson claims he had a fish on his hook and that he had himself a prizewinner for sure, had the fish almost out of the water, when a naked woman came out of the water and yanked the fishing pole out of his hands."

Shane grinned. "A naked woman? Where did you say he liked to fish?"

Aimee sighed. "Pig."

"Oink."

"Anyway." Their father's tone was mildly exasperated. "There's a lot of weirdness going on and no one has a decent explanation."

"Did you hear anything about a tree that talks?" Aimee asked.

Her dad scrunched his eyebrows together. "No . . . can't say that I have. What's the story on that?"

Shane spoke up quickly, much to Aimee's annoyance. "Just some stuff going around the school. There's supposed to be an oak tree in the woods that moves from place to place. It's like, you can't see it if you're looking for it, but if you aren't looking for it, it's there."

"It's supposed to talk to people," Aimee cut in, eager to finish the story herself. "Like, it's supposed to tell you secrets and even things about the future."

Their father smiled. "Yeah, and when I was a kid, there was a covered bridge where they said the locals used to hang people, and if you went there during the full moon, you could see their ghosts. Don't put too much stock in that sort of stuff. Look, I have to run to work and you two have to get to school." His face softened as he spoke, his eyes crinkling at the corners, and he reached over to give her shoulder a squeeze. She knew he was trying to let her know that he loved her, even if he didn't always understand her.

That was okay. The feeling was mutual.

Shane and Aimee walked in silence, heading down Main Street toward school. They could have asked for a ride, could maybe even have gotten the bus if they could figure out where the stop was, but both of them were used to walking in Boston.

"So what do you think about the tree?" Aimee sounded a little breathless, so Shane slowed down a bit. It wasn't like he was in a rush; he just normally walked fast.

Shane shrugged. "I dunno. It's definitely weird that so many people say they've seen it. I can tell you one thing, though—Dad couldn't care less about talking trees."

"Yeah. I sort of got that." She looked at the ground and shook her head. "I thought he'd want to know. I mean, it's news, isn't it? No matter what the truth is?"

"Maybe not to Dad." He looked over at his sister and studied her for a second. Sometimes she looked so young to him and other times like she could be in college. Right now, with her dark brown hair in a ponytail, her eyes wide, and her mouth stuck in a sullen frown, she seemed like a five-year-old version of herself. And so, so sad. It was an expression he'd seen so many—*too* many—times since their mother had died. "You know how he is," he went on, pulling himself out of his thoughts. "If something isn't solid, if you can't hold it in your hands or prove it on paper, it doesn't exist. He was the one who told us Santa Claus wasn't real and the Easter Bunny didn't really deliver the baskets. Mom would have probably kept us going for another five years at least."

She nodded but didn't speak right away. Just to kill the silence, he spoke himself. "What I want to know is what was up with those cats."

Aimee rubbed her hands over her arms. He could see the gooseflesh crawl over her skin as she thought about the cats and their savage attack on the old lady who owned them. "I feel sorry for her. I saw Dad's notes on the table. They had to practically sew her ear back on."

"Maybe she should have sicced Hizzoner on them."

Aimee laughed lightly for a second before sobering. "What do you think Hizzoner is?" She looked his way, her eyes bright with curiosity. "Maybe it's a ghost. I mean, it hasn't actually hurt anyone so far."

With all the crazy stories going around town, they'd somehow managed to avoid talking about what they really believed. Aimee knew Shane was interested in ghosts and stuff like that, and she'd teased him about it in the past. But he didn't think she was teasing now. The thing was, Shane wasn't sure what he thought about the black dog, whether it was a ghost or a bear or some bogeyman. Or bogey-dog.

"No, it hasn't hurt anyone yet. But I think it's tried a few times."

"Can ghosts hurt people?"

Shane shrugged. "Never met one."

"Hey there," came a voice from behind them.

Shane glanced over his shoulder to see Stasia hurrying to catch up to them. He smiled, she returned the smile, and something warm and fuzzy filled his chest. It was hard to believe any girl could look that good. Stasia wore low-rider jeans and a baby tee with the word *Temptress* written across it in glittering cursive. Her hair was down and the way the wind caught it made her look like a model at a fashion shoot, only without the four pounds of makeup.

He made himself look away. It would be rude to stare, and it would also be bad if Aimee caught him ogling her new best bud—so far her only bud, really. The two had definitely been getting close since they'd all met that first day. Whenever he saw Aimee in the halls at school, Stasia seemed to be right there with her.

"You guys mind a little company?"

Before Shane could open his mouth, Aimee was talking, asking Stasia what she thought about the whole business with the whispering oak tree and Hizzoner.

"If it looks like a tree, feels like a tree, and smells like a tree, it's probably a tree. In this case, it's just a tree that does other things, too."

Shane blinked, not certain he'd heard right. "So you think the tree is real?"

Stasia flipped her hair back. "Why not? There are a

lot of strange things out there." Her eyes grew distant for a second.

Aimee smiled victoriously. "See? I knew I couldn't be the only one."

"I never said I didn't think it was possible," Shane said. "I would just like more proof."

"You've been hanging around Dad too much," Aimee grumbled.

Stasia came to his rescue. "Your dad's a reporter. He's supposed to be skeptical." She arched one eyebrow and looked at Aimee. "Besides, it never hurts to know all you can before you make a decision."

"But you said you thought the whispering tree was real," Aimee said, narrowing her eyes.

"That doesn't mean I'm right."

Shane sighed. "Listen, I'd love to believe in all this stuff. Seriously. But in my whole life I've never seen anything that breaks the rules the rest of the world tells us to believe. Until I do . . . If all these crazy things are really going on in this town, how come no one has any concrete evidence? Until someone comes up with something, y'know, tangible, you have to figure there's a logical explanation for everything."

Stasia shrugged. "Define logic. There've been stories of ghosts and goblins and everything else for thousands of years. All over the world. Those stories wouldn't be so widespread if there wasn't a grain of truth in there somewhere. Just because you haven't seen the tree, you think it doesn't exist. I know at least ten kids at school who say they've seen it. Or heard it or whatever."

Shane didn't have a response for that.

"Okay," Aimee said, "but you've lived here all your life. Have you ever seen anything to make you believe in this stuff? Ever seen the big dog or the tree? No."

Aimee had added the no without waiting for Stasia to respond. Just for a moment, though, Stasia had glanced at the ground and Shane wondered if she'd been considering a different answer.

"Well, there've always been stories," she said. "I mean, come on, it's Sleepy Hollow. As in 'Legend Of'? We're the original creepy American town. But most of it's just myth or people's imagination. Or at least it used to be. . . . If so many people are experiencing this stuff suddenly, maybe it isn't just the loonies anymore."

Shane studied her. "You really believe all of this?"

"I keep an open mind."

He nodded. "Okay. Let's say I believe it. Which I don't, but let's say I do. Why here? Why Sleepy Hollow?"

Aimee shot him an impatient look. "Didn't you just hear her? Sleepy Hollow's always had legends. There's Hizzoner. Not to mention the . . . whaddayoucallim? The Headless Horseman."

"Okay. So answer me this. Why now?"

Stasia shrugged. "Beats me."

She laughed and the conversation moved on. But Shane was left with two clear thoughts in his mind.

One, he had to learn more about the local legends of Sleepy Hollow, because *something* really strange was happening.

Two, he had been absolutely right about Stasia Traeger. She was as intelligent as she was gorgeous.

Shane spent most of the day trying not to think about her and failing miserably.

It was the start of their second week at Sleepy Hollow High, and Aimee was finally deciding she sort of liked their new school. She'd already made a few friends, especially Stasia, and there were at least a dozen guys who made it a point to say hi to her whenever they could. She wasn't really looking for a boyfriend, but it was nice to be noticed.

Of course there were downsides to everything. The most significant at the present moment was the report she was currently trying to research, sitting in the public library with her brother. Much as she kept trying to focus on the books she'd selected earlier, her mind kept wandering. Every time she even saw a tree, she started thinking about the "magic" oak out in the woods. A truth-telling tree seemed pretty cool, but everyone who had allegedly encountered the tree had ended up hurt by what they heard.

Shane didn't seem to have a problem concentrating on his work. He was flipping from book to book and taking notes as if the fate of the world depended on the answers. He didn't just do homework; he attacked it. Sometimes she envied him that ability, but mostly she just wished he'd get a real social life. Already he was hanging with Jekyll and Hyde, and they seemed nice enough, but they weren't exactly going to win him access to the inner circles of high school society—especially Steve.

A shadow blocked her light, and Aimee looked up, a bit spooked. She let out her breath, feeling silly when she recognized Mr. Mickle, the librarian. Like the Warner Public Library, where they were doing their research, he almost seemed like he belonged to a different time. He had the face of a vulture, all wrinkles and a big beak of a nose, but he was also about as friendly as any of the adults she'd run across in town. The library had closed over an hour ago, but he'd let them stay to work on their papers.

He flashed an apologetic smile. "Okay, kids. I have to kick you out. I'm ready to head home."

Shane jerked up his head, his brow furrowing in obvious disappointment.

"Thanks, Mr. Mickle," Aimee said. "We really appreciate you letting us stay so late."

"Well, just make sure you get an A on those papers."

Shane shoved his notebook into his book bag, nodded his thanks, and started for the door. As she followed him, Aimee heard a loud creak from up in the children's section and craned her head to see if she'd hear anything else. There was nothing, but for an instant she got a flash of cold between her shoulders and shivered. *Just an old building, that's all.* Shane and the librarian were already at the door, waiting. She jogged up to them.

Two minutes later they were on their way home, Shane still acting like he was coming out of a deep sleep. Sometimes it seemed to her that studying was like swimming in the deep end of the pool for her brother. He got himself so lost in the work that he could drown if he wasn't careful.

Henry Mickle watched the kids go and smiled. He envied them their youth, but not what they were probably going through every day of their young lives. He remembered being that age well enough, and it seemed like everything back in those days had been a major event. Never any small troubles, just epic dilemmas.

Time to lock up now. All he needed to do was one more check of the building before he shut down the lights and turned on the security system. Henry drank in the scent of books and smiled contentedly.

And then he heard the sound.

It wasn't loud, but it didn't belong. After nearly forty years working in the library, he knew every sound there was to hear. Something upstairs in the Kiddie Corner was moving around. Something a lot bigger than a mouse.

"If anyone's up there, we've been closed for a while and I'm about to set the alarms. It's time to leave." He felt like a fool calling out, but at least anyone coming along would know that he was there, and they'd be ready to leave by the time he got to the top of the stairs. *Unless of course they want to rob you, Henry.*

That was a nonsense idea if ever there was one. Nobody robbed libraries, and even if they did, they didn't expect to get much beyond a few books and maybe fifty dollars in late fines. Still, something had him on edge.

The library echoed with several resonating thumps that made the mezzanine above him shudder. The loud thuds moved toward the stairs leading down, and Henry felt a twinge of fear slither through his stomach.

He looked up the stairs and felt much, much smaller than he usually did. Henry had to actually rub his eyes to make sure he wasn't seeing things. It wasn't possible, of course. He was old and his mind was playing tricks on him. Had to be.

Had to be.

Too many books, too many Halloweens, too many children to be read to. And this town, of course.

There was no way he was really seeing a horse and rider up in the shadows of the second floor. No way. Because if it was really there, well, then he would have to scream, and if his mind hadn't snapped already, it just might.

Then it moved, slowly, hooves thumping the floor, coming to the top of the stairs. And there was something not quite right about the rider. *No,* he thought. *It's a trick of the light. Or of the shadows.*

The horse was heavily muscled and jet black, with a thick, lustrous hide and a wild mane. The rider sat with gloved hands on the reins and didn't make a sound. The animal let out a snort of impatience and pranced a little at the edge of the second-story loft.

Henry moved, hurrying toward the main desk, and had almost reached the phone when he heard the sudden rattle of reins and rustle of leather. He looked back just in time to see the stallion rear up and launch itself down toward him, hooves thundering on the stairs. Old Mr. Mickle didn't even scream; he just ran. Ran and prayed.

The horse and rider hit the carpeted floor of the library, scattering displays of magazines across half the lobby and regaining balance with uncanny ease. The librarian let out a moan of fear and darted toward the main desk again, hoping to get past the massive wooden kiosk and all the way to the offices in the back of the lower level. He glanced back at the moving insanity behind him, hoping frantically that he would make it to the relative safety of the wooden shelter.

The black steed bulldozed a table out of its way, hitting it with enough force to flip the heavy obstacle. The crash was deafening. Henry changed tactics when a chair from near the table rolled past him. It might not be heavy enough to stop the horse's progress, but it was likely the best weapon he was going to get his hands on.

As if he'd been waiting for a cue, the Horseman reached to his waist and drew a sword that had rested in a scabbard at his hip. He made no sound, but the metal of the blade sang as it kissed the air.

With nowhere else to go, Henry dove for the closest table, fully aware that it wasn't adequate shelter. The black warhorse knocked him aside as casually as he would move a house cat, and Henry rolled across the floor, colliding with several chairs in the process. Something in his left elbow snapped with a white-hot flare of pain, and for a second everything went gray.

When the world came back into focus, the rider was leaning down on his horse and gripping the table Henry was resting beneath. He flipped the massive thing easily out of his way, and Henry stared up at his attacker, lit by the harsh fluorescent lights.

At last he screamed, forgetting every ache and pain in his body and pushing himself off the ground with the energy of a child. He ran, blindly shoving past every obstacle, determined to get away from the nightmare charging after him on horseback.

Iron-shod hooves pounded the carpeting behind him, cutting through the weave down to the insulation below. Henry ran as fast as he could for the front doors of the library, praying desperately for salvation. The dark horse screamed behind him, almost masking the sound of the sword that carved the air as it aimed for his neck.

"You'd forget your head if it wasn't glued on," Shane snapped at Aimee as they doubled back toward the library. Why did he always have to be such a brat? So she'd left a book behind; it wasn't the end of the world. They hadn't gotten very far and Mr. Mickle was probably still there, closing up.

"Anyone ever tell you that you talk like an old man, Shane?"

"Anyone ever tell you to get a clue?" Shane smirked. "Or maybe a brain that still works?"

They rounded a corner and the library came into sight, the lights still on inside. "I think he's here," Aimee said, walking faster. She looked at the front doors as they approached. Through the small glass panes set at eye level she could see movement, shadows playing on the wall near the hallway leading into the main lobby. "Thank God! I really need that book."

"Drama queen. Let's just hope he isn't pissed."

Shane was reaching out to knock on the double doors when they heard the sounds from inside the building, deep rhythmic, resonating booms that thundered closer at high speed. The doors slammed open with enough force to shatter the glass panes and knock Shane back onto the sidewalk. He barely had time to let out a grunt of surprise before a massive black thing was on them.

At first all she could see was the dark shape, large and moving fast. Aimee looked up as it pushed through the entranceway of the library. Somewhere on the other side of the thing her brother let out a gasp of pain, but she couldn't see him past the shadowy form. Her eyes tracked a boot and a leg, then higher to the body of a man in ancient, dusty clothing. And from there she saw the man's arm and what he held in his grasp as it swayed back and forth.

The horse looked at her with one eye, its head lifting and shaking side to side.

Shane scrambled backward, fingers scraping concrete as the midnight black animal stomped a hoof down where he had been a second before, sparks flashing from the impact. It reared into the air, the rider so high above them that Aimee had a clear view only of his riding boots. She let out a scream that was piercing even to her own ears and backpedaled as the horse came down again, then leaped in her direction. She threw herself to one side, falling hard, knocking the air out of her lungs.

The rider dropped its grisly prize. It struck the earth next to the concrete path with a wet thump. Then horse and horseman thundered across the lawn and into the parking lot of the library before charging down Main Street.

For a second Aimee stared after them. She turned

her head sharply when she heard Shane's sudden explosive scream. He scrambled up to his feet and backed away, his eyes wide and his face pale. She followed his gaze to a spot just a couple of feet away from where she had landed on the ground.

Aimee looked at the bloody, severed head of Henry Mickle, its eyes wide with terror, and gasped sharply. A terrible screeching filled the air, and she wondered numbly where it came from. She only realized the sound was coming from her own lips when she sucked in a breath and started screaming again.

CHAPTER FIVE

SHANE TRIED TO sip his coffee—*decaf, thanks, ha ha, isn't that a scream? Just like when Aimee started screaming*—and watched the hot liquid dance inside the cup from the way his hands were twitching. Every time he closed his eyes even for a second, he saw the head of the librarian roll across the ground and land by Aimee's feet. The head had rolled and bounced, and every time it bounced, it seemed to him that the dead man's eyes had accused him of something.

Aimee sat next to him instead of across the table. He put one nervous arm around her and felt her shiver before she leaned in closer.

"I can't believe this. It has to be a nightmare." Aimee's voice was thin and shaky.

"I wish it was." Shane managed to sip his coffee without spilling it all over himself and then set it down, afraid to tempt fate any longer. He didn't want to be here. He wanted to be at home, back in his old room in Boston, safely under the sheets and hiding, like when he was a little kid and stayed up late to watch a scary movie. He desperately wished that his mom would come in and tell him it was all just make-believe, but of course that wasn't going to happen.

Aimee let out a shuddery breath and reached for her hot cocoa. They were sitting in the Muffin Man, across from the library. Aimee was still shaken and he couldn't blame her. He felt like he'd had his entire stomach turned inside out.

And then there was Dad. Dad wasn't exactly upset; more like horrified. When Shane and Aimee had recovered enough from the shock of what they'd seen to even begin to think, they'd rushed into the library to use the phone. Shane had called the police station first and then their father.

Their dad had freaked out, but as soon as he confirmed that Shane and Aimee were all right, he had told them to get to the Muffin Man. Shane hadn't been completely in control of his thoughts yet. He had, in fact, still been thinking about the night-black horse that almost ran him down and the rolling head of Henry Mickle with its wide, staring eyes. Even so, he offered to stay there and wait for the cops, even when Aimee started to cry, unable to stop looking at the decapitated corpse on the floor, and his father had screamed at him to get the hell away from the library because the killer might come back. So Shane and Aimee were waiting for their father, looking at the crime scene and watching the police department crawl over the area.

The worst part was, there was a morbid part of Shane that wanted to see the head again, just to make sure it was real. He'd seen the blood and steam that rose from the cleanly cut throat just below the old man's jawline, smelled the metallic tang that rose from the stump, and seen the way the nerves in the head made the facial muscles twitch, but there was some piece of him that wouldn't believe it unless he saw it again.

Yet maybe that was for the best, pretending to himself that it was just some special effect, like in the movies.

Or maybe not. He was going to have to go back to the crime scene just as soon as his dad gave him a call on the cell phone. The very idea sent ice rolling across his skin. With his free arm he took another sip of coffee, barely noticing when it spilled across his hand.

"You okay, Aimee?" he asked.

"No. How could I be?" Her voice was a little petulant, which was at least an improvement over the sheer terror that had dominated her tone since they'd sat down, but it still seemed out of line, considering he was only trying to help.

"Excuse me for caring," he snapped, on instinct.

"Whatever."

Shane pulled his arm from around her shoulders and noticed the wounded look she got on her face. He knew he should apologize, put his arm back around her, and let it go, but he just couldn't deal with her attitude right now.

The door to the restaurant opened and their father came in. Aimee was up instantly and running to him, crying again, wrapping her thin arms around his waist, and he was holding her and comforting her. As Shane got up and went over, their father was assuring her everything would be okay.

Chief Burroughs came in a moment later and Shane and Aimee sat back down at the table with him and with their father, and the questions started. It took ages, but Shane didn't mind. At least he didn't have to be alone.

Shane sat back and stretched, feeling the muscles in his neck and shoulders protest the sudden change of position. He'd finished the stupid paper. He should have been relieved, but instead he concentrated on what to work on next. If he kept himself busy enough, he wouldn't have to think. It was a trick he'd learned a long time ago—a busy mind doesn't have time to wander or to dwell on things like . . .

Mom.

Or watching a dead man's head roll across the concrete, spilling black blood.

Or the girl he couldn't get out of his thoughts even when he knew she could bring him nothing but trouble. Stasia Traeger was out of his league and so far away from what he considered his safety zone that he was sure to get singed just coming close to her. But he kept looking forward to when Aimee would bring her over, and he kept thinking about her dozen different ways to smile and how every expression she made, every time her eyes locked with his, every time he heard her light, carefree laugh made him feel like he couldn't catch his breath.

It was pleasant and it was torture and he craved her presence like she was his own personal drug habit. He'd dreamed about her the other night. It had started off steamy, the sort of dream that would leave him waking up edgy and frustrated, and become a nightmare when he'd touched her hair and her head had fallen off, rolling across the hardwood floor of his bedroom.

He didn't scream when he woke up from that one, but it was close.

Shane shook his head. There were plenty of girls at school. Maybe if he tried hard enough, he could find a different one to obsess over. Stasia had no interest in him, and even if she did, she was Aimee's friend and he knew that kind of thing was off-limits. He'd learned that little rule in Boston.

Still . . .

He shook his head again and saved the file for his report on colonial New York and the history of the Hudson Valley. Working on the paper had started him thinking again about Stasia's comments about Sleepy

Hollow and local legends. Remembering the promise he'd made to himself, he signed on to his Internet connection and started a Google search for black dogs and hell hounds. He figured that was as good a place to start as any.

"Your dad's going to be pissed, isn't he?" Stasia whispered in Aimee's ear.

"No, he's cool about this sort of stuff. Besides, it's not like we're out partying. It's just having you stay over."

"No, I mean about you being out so late."

Aimee looked at Stasia. Her friend had dyed her hair with streaks of dark blue and red that should have looked goofy but somehow worked on her. Stasia gnawed lightly on her bottom lip. Aimee appreciated her friend's concern but wasn't worried. Her dad would deal. She had moved to the stupid town for him, and she figured he could handle her being late now and again.

She walked up the stairs to the front door and opened it, gesturing for Stasia to stay in the foyer while she went in and confronted her father.

He was in the living room, looking over the day's *Gazette,* probably searching for typos. His eyebrows were knit closely and his foot wiggled where he sat, a sure sign that he was worried.

"Hi, Daddy." She put on her most apologetic smile, hoping to win him over before things could get out of hand.

"It's pretty late, Aimee. Where have you been?" His voice didn't sound as forgiving as she'd hoped.

"I was just out, over at Stasia's."

"You know our cell phone plan makes it easy for you to call home and let me know when you're going to be . . ." He looked at his watch. "Almost ninety minutes late."

She threw out an exaggerated sigh. "Dad . . ."

"No, Aimee. I don't want to hear about how old you are. I want to know why you were an hour and a half late coming home and why you didn't bother to call to let me know you were going to be late." His voice was more than a little strained. "After what happened . . . after the other night I need you to call. I'm not going to let it slide anymore. I need to know you're safe."

"I lost track of the time, and my cell phone battery died. I was going to call, but I didn't think to until I was already on my way here."

Her father looked at her long and hard, trying to decide whether or not she was lying. She was, of course, but he didn't need to know that. Aimee wasn't the type to lie about anything important, but a little white one now and then to smooth things over just seemed like common sense to her.

"Fine." He shrugged. "But save me a heart attack, will you? I can't handle . . . Look, next time you pull a stunt like this, it's going to cost you your freedom for a week. This time I let you off with a warning."

"Come on, Dad . . ." She rolled her eyes toward

the ceiling. "When did you turn into such a hardass?"

"No, Aimee, *you* come on! Somebody out there cut off a man's head four nights ago! Whoever did that hasn't been caught! And for all I know he saw your face or Shane's. What if he's worried you saw *him?*"

She flinched. Try though she might, she couldn't seem to escape hearing about the beheading—and she was trying very, very hard. Did he really think it hadn't occurred to her that she'd been a witness? That she could be the next target? Didn't he get that was the whole *point*, pushing that thought as far out of her mind as possible?

Her father winced and moved toward her. "What am I supposed to think when you're this late and don't call?" he said, his voice softer.

"You're right. I'm sorry."

He took another step forward and she gave him a quick hug, then stepped back to look him in the eyes. "Listen, on kind of the same subject, Stasia's folks are both working tonight and I was hoping she could spend the night here."

"It's a school night, Aimee."

"I know, but—"

"And I have to be honest: I think you are spending a little too much time away from home or with your friends and not enough time on your homework."

She hated when he used that card, mainly because it was true on more than one count. She *had* been spending a lot of time away from the house, though she did have reasons, even if she couldn't share them with her father. And as far as the homework was concerned . . . she couldn't even lie about that, just in case he checked on her. So she covered with a bit of truth.

"I've almost got my report finished," she offered.

"Can I read it?"

"I said almost. It's not finished yet, but it will be."

"Aimee, your friend can't stay over. I'm sorry, but you have school tomorrow, and I'm sure you have work you should be doing."

"Dad, come on!"

"Aimee, you just broke curfew—do you really think now is a good time to argue with me?" His voice got louder and he pressed his lips together into a thin white line that said he'd get into a full screaming match if he had to.

She dropped her voice. "Dad, she's already here and I can't make her walk home alone. Besides, she's kind of freaked to be at her house by herself, you know?"

Her father looked at her, his eyes dark and angry, and at the same time she could see him mulling it over in his head. "Fine," he finally said. "She can stay the night."

"Thank you." She started to turn away.

"But I want to see the first draft of your paper ready for me to read in the morning, or you and I will have a long talk about this."

That pretty much shut down the celebration. She

nodded somberly, ready to print up and copy a report from the Internet. It would hardly be the first time she'd cut corners. As long as she could add on a bibliography that looked legitimate, she'd be fine.

"Absolutely."

Aimee beckoned Stasia inside. They headed up the stairs, planning by unspoken agreement to keep quiet until they got to her room.

Naturally Shane came along and screwed that up. He was standing in his bedroom door, directly across from her room, with his face set and angry. "Yeah, that's good, Aimee. Add to Dad's troubles with a fight or two."

Aimee glared at him and moved forward. He looked past her and saw Stasia for the first time and blanched like he'd just realized he wasn't wearing any pants, which, happily, he was.

"Mind your own business, Shane."

Shane stepped into the hallway, blocking her progress. "It *is* my business. You need to stop giving him grief. He's been through enough, not to mention the new job and all." He was still in fight mode, but he was keeping it down to just above a whisper.

Aimee rolled her eyes again and scowled. "You think I don't know what he's been through?"

"I know your phone is charged—I saw you using it earlier. Next time just call him instead of acting like a brat."

"You need to know what you're talking about before

you open your big, fat mouth, Shane." She kept her voice low too, but it wasn't easy for her.

"What do you mean by that?"

"Nothing!" Aimee stomped into her room, pushing past her brother, waiting for Stasia to follow her.

Shane looked at Stasia and swallowed hard. She smiled awkwardly, her eyes wide and almost hypnotic, and waved her delicate fingers as she slid past him to get into Aimee's room. And just like that all of his righteous anger blew away like fog in a hard wind and he had to remember to breathe. Truth be told, half the reason he was angry was because Stasia was staying across the hallway from him for the night. Like there was any chance he was going to sleep now.

Derek Van Brunt walked home from the party, feeling the effects of too much celebration and too little sleep but not minding. They'd won against the Tarrytown team, and it felt good to win. He was pumped about the game. And the fact that he could still taste Erin Ingalsby's breath mints on his lips wasn't exactly hurting.

He cut across the cornfield at the edge of the Ingalsby property. The breeze was light and chilly and his letterman's jacket barely seemed enough to keep out the cold. Behind him, not very far away, something pushed against the cornstalks and he heard them rustle, snapping in the breeze and shaking. The sound was so unexpected that Derek froze.

The sound came again, closer and louder, and he thought about the big black dog that Kyle Murphy said had chased him halfway across town. Kyle wasn't the only one with stories about the thing, either. Then he thought about Mr. Mickle's murder.

He started running. Behind him the corn shook and he heard the sound of several of the heavy stalks being knocked aside. Mr. Ingalsby was going to be really, really ticked off.

Derek dodged through the rows of corn, moving as fast as he dared on the soft soil. Just up ahead he could see the low stone wall that separated his family's property from the Ingalsbys'. His foot hooked a thick stalk of corn in the darkness and he screamed, almost falling but stumbling instead, waving his arms and hopping from one leg to the other as his momentum carried him along. He dared a look behind him but saw only that whatever was chasing him through the corn was much, much closer now.

Derek let out a stream of curses and ran, arms pumping, legs pistoning, and head down, his one goal in the world simply to get over the wall and into a clearer area. His lungs burned and his breath plumed in the cold autumn air.

To his left the corn jumped, uprooted by the force of whatever was hitting it, and to the right the almost-constant hiss of the corn leaves rattling was enough to

73

make his hair stand on end. Just ahead of him was the four-foot-high stone wall.

He jumped, his feet leaving the ground just as something brushed his left ankle. He braced himself, sure that he was going to shatter his kneecaps against the wall or hook his foot and hit the other side so hard his neck would snap. His feet danced in the air, seeking something to land on, and he got lucky, his left sneaker touching down on the top of the wall.

As he landed on the other side, his feet slid in the dew-damp grass and went out from under him. He went down on his back, sliding another dozen feet before he could stop his forward momentum.

He rolled onto his stomach and looked back at the stone wall. He saw the tops of the cornstalks shuddering violently, not in one or two places but in a hundred. Derek got to his feet. He could see over the low wall. The grass at the edge of the Ingalsby property rustled and shivered as though that too were being pushed aside. Something was moving the grass, moving the corn, but he couldn't see what it was.

It hit the wall from the cornfield side, and Derek jumped back as the impact loosened stones that had been in the same place for centuries. The wall bulged out as if it might collapse, but the stones didn't fall.

Derek's breath came out in ragged gasps and his heart felt like it was trying to break out of his chest. He stared at the wall, his eyes wide, too stunned by what he'd seen to move. He knew he was a dead man. Whatever could do that to the wall would have no problem getting over it or coming right through it.

But nothing else happened. Whatever was over there, either it didn't want to come after him or it couldn't. He walked backward, terrified to take his eyes from the wall and the cornfield beyond, and slowly moved across the lawn to his own house. He didn't turn around until he made it to the front door.

CHAPTER
SIX

SHANE STARED ACROSS the table at Aimee, his bio lab partner. She'd been in a mood all morning, but at least that was finally changing. Jekyll and Hyde, also partners, were sitting a few seats down the long lab table that half the class was seated around. Jekyll was currently leering good-naturedly at Aimee, trying to break her out of her funk. It seemed to be working—as much as she tried to look appropriately disgusted, there was a twinkle in her eyes that showed she was struggling not to laugh.

Meanwhile Mark Hyde was doodling away in his notebook. If it was like the rest of his scribbled pictures, it was probably either a metal band logo or something obscene. Today his shirt bore the cover of a Mushroomhead CD. His head was cocked and he was listening to Derek Van Brunt talk about his adventures the night before. Something about being attacked at the Ingalsbys' farm. All Shane knew for sure was that Derek looked particularly ugly that morning, with a few scratches on his face. Derek was just finishing the story of how he'd jumped a wall between their yards, and much as Shane wanted to paint the jock as a complete idiot, the guy didn't sound like he was bragging so much as recovering from a bad scene.

Alicia D'Agostino—not Shane's type and therefore safe from his search for a new obsession, but thanks for playing—jumped in next, talking about how her sister, Andrea, had actually been to the whispering tree. Alicia's dark eyes were wide and her baby face looked a little slack as she spoke. "Andrea says it tells you secrets, all right, but not the kind you want to know. She said it told her Carla was sneaking around with Robby. Her best friend and her boyfriend! And you know what? She caught them together two days later getting all busy under the bleachers after school."

Mark Hyde nodded knowingly but didn't say a word. He almost never spoke in class. It seemed that when he did, people got worried. Most people were inclined to flinch when he spoke in their direction. Shane had to wonder just how rough a bully his friend used to be.

Jekyll wasn't as quiet. "Yeah, Mark saw that go down. Your sister isn't a girl to be trifled with." He shrugged. "She's also not the only one I've heard about who saw the tree."

"Who else?" Alicia frowned.

"Kevin Hamburg, Patsy Lopez, and Kristin Barrington. At least. Maybe more." He shrugged. "I don't think any of them are lying."

When this kind of thing had come up the previous week, Derek Van Brunt had scoffed and made some nasty comments. Shane looked in the jock's direction, but Derek had nothing to say this time. He merely listened, his face pale.

Aimee listened raptly. She didn't volunteer anything, but she was paying attention to every detail.

"I hear that it moves from place to place and that the only way you can find it is to not be looking for it," Steve said. "Kristin went looking for it the next day after she saw it and couldn't find it, even though she found the landmarks she'd used to nail where it had been."

Mark narrowed his eyes at Aimee, finally joining the conversation. "Hey, at least it isn't cutting off heads."

Aimee looked at Mark, taken aback. Shane was just as surprised—he'd told Mark how sensitive Aimee was about what had happened.

Bill Hastings nodded. "Yeah. My uncle Cyrus thinks the Headless Horseman is back in town."

Mark smiled thinly. "Let's be fair. Your uncle Cyrus isn't exactly the most reliable source. . . ."

Bill nodded and lowered his head. Shane had only been in town for about three weeks, but even he had heard about Cyrus Hastings. Apparently Cyrus's blood was around forty proof.

Like a mouse chastising a lion, Steve reached out a fast hand and slapped Mark on the back of the head.

The blow wasn't exactly brutal, but it wasn't light either. Hyde glared at his personal Jekyll for a second and then immediately shot an apologetic glance at Bill.

All around the room the tension level had built, but Shane didn't think it was just because of Hyde's harsh contributions to the conversation. He made a note to check out the tree story at the school library. The idea of going to the other library wasn't sitting comfortably just yet—go figure.

Aimee waved her hand in a dismissive gesture. "Just 'cause some fruit bat with a sword is cutting off heads doesn't mean that he didn't have a head himself." Her words were blasé and they might have fooled most of the kids in the bio lab, but Shane knew better. "No one believes ghosts are real anyway."

This time it was Steve who looked at her. "You sure about that, Aimee?"

"What do you mean?" She blinked.

"I mean maybe when she gets back from talking to Mr. Hurwitz about that test she missed, you should talk to Stasia about ghosts and goblins."

"Why?" Her tone was guarded, suspicious, and Shane wondered why, after the conversation they'd had on the topic with Stasia the other day.

"If there's anyone who comes close to being an expert on things that go bump in the night around here, everyone knows it's Stasia Traeger," Steve replied.

Shane was ready to ask for more info, but before he

could speak, their teacher, Ms. Dimitrios, cleared her throat. Normally she didn't care if they talked in class as long as they got their experiments done. Today she'd apparently reached her limit. "That's enough nonsense. Next person I hear mentioning monsters in my class is getting detention."

It was much, much later in the night when Aimee finally got to ask Stasia about what Jekyll and Hyde had said. They were out in the woods, with only the light from a few lanterns to keep the darkness at bay. All told there were around nine kids sitting on or near four cars, and there was at least a case of empty beer bottles around them. Most of the people there were in college. Aimee and Stasia were the only exceptions, and while they'd been having a good time, Aimee was buzzed enough to be comfortable but not stupid. The sweet smell of marijuana filled the air. Aimee liked the smell and didn't mind breathing it in, though she wasn't going to smoke it.

The music was by a band she'd never heard before, but she liked it. Stasia was enjoying it even more. So far she'd been dancing up against just about every guy there, and half of them looked like they wanted to do a lot more than dance with her. Everything about Stasia exuded a raw sexuality that fascinated Aimee. But for the most part Stasia seemed deliberately oblivious to the drooling looks the guys gave her.

Aimee wasn't dancing that closely with any of the

guys—though there were a couple who made her want to—but she was drawing plenty of looks herself. She took her cue from Stasia and did her best to ignore them. After the current song ended, Stasia grabbed another beer and moved with that unsettling grace of hers over to where Aimee was sitting this one out.

"We should get matching tattoos," Stasia remarked.

"Excuse me?"

"Matching tattoos," Stasia explained calmly. "We should get some. Something small that most people would never see."

"We could maybe do that, Stasia, but not tonight."

"Well, we could tonight, but I think it'd be better if we decided what we were going to get first."

Aimee laughed. "Can I ask you something?"

"You just did, but you can even ask me another question." Stasia tipped back her beer.

"Jekyll and Hyde said you're kind of a local expert on spooky stuff. Is that true?"

Stasia looked over at the boys sitting around. Without her to dance with, they had resorted to leaning on cars or milling about, talking over whatever it was college guys discussed when getting drunk.

"Spooky stuff? Is that the technical term?"

Aimee frowned. "I'm serious."

Stasia sighed and looked south at the lights of the Tappan Zee Bridge where it rose above the tree line in the distance. "Yeah, I guess you could say it's a hobby of mine."

"Why didn't you say anything? I mean, with all the weirdness going on around here and that whole conversation we had the other day."

Stasia looked at her with a deadpan face. "I thought I did say something. Maybe you weren't paying attention. Besides, I didn't think it was a big deal."

"Okay, we spent the last couple of nights—"

"Hey, Stasia! Come dance with me!" The voice of Todd Harper cut through Aimee's words. He leaned on the hood of the car, his beefy arms practically a barrier between her and Stasia. He reeked of beer. Aimee and Stasia had both had a couple of drinks, but the guys they were hanging with were knocking the booze down like fish drink water. Without even bothering to look her way, Todd slid a hand up Aimee's knee and squeezed.

Aimee pulled back. He was a cute enough blockhead, but she barely knew him, and letting Todd get all grabby wasn't really in her plans for the night. Todd said something to Stasia that Aimee didn't hear, and her friend laughed, shaking her head.

They both had school in the morning, and it was almost 11 P.M. Her dad was working late at the paper, but that didn't mean he might not drop by for a sneak inspection. Maybe the beer was making her paranoid or maybe it was the fact that most of the guys around them were close to pickled and looking at her and at Stasia with a creepy sort of stare. Either way, it was time to go home.

Stasia slid off the hood of the vehicle they'd been

perched on and started dancing against Todd. Todd looked a little like he'd died and gone to heaven as he started moving with her, their bodies brushing each other's.

"We should get out of here, Stasia." She spoke just loud enough for Stasia to hear her over the boom of the music.

Stasia only smiled. "It's early."

Shane paced the floor. Aimee was acting like a little brat, and if he wasn't so worried about his dad being worried about her, he'd have just narced her out when his father called instead of making excuses for her. Sooner or later her father was bound to catch on to what she was pulling, but until then Shane was going to do his best to make sure Alan Lancaster stayed ignorant.

The newspaper was a lot more work than his father had expected. Shane could tell just by the hours his father was keeping. The way he came home dragging almost every night was another sure sign. Part of it was definitely all the weirdness in town, events that required more actual reporting for a newspaper in a town that usually had little news. And part of it was that as his father had said, he'd underestimated just how "part-time" most of the part-timers were. They were basically useless. Except for the final layout and sending the paper off to the printer, Alan was responsible for nearly every aspect of the *Sleepy Hollow Gazette*'s publication.

So Shane told a few lies to preserve Alan's peace of mind. That didn't make him feel good about it.

Aimee breezed through the front door just shy of midnight, obviously confident that she was home free since their dad's car wasn't in the driveway.

Shane didn't give her a chance to get comfortable. He just jumped right in. "You think maybe you could call when you're going to be stupid?"

Aimee reeled back. "What? What do you mean?"

"I mean I've had to lie to Dad four times tonight about where you are. If I had to tell him you were in the bathroom one more time, he'd have called for an ambulance." Okay, he was exaggerating. Their father had called twice. That wasn't the point.

Aimee wasn't in the mood for learning any lessons, apparently, because she shook her head and then moved to walk past him. "Whatever. Dad isn't here, so there's no problem. Get over yourself."

"I'm serious, Aimee. I'm not covering for you anymore. You can tell your own lies to Dad when he decides to bust you."

She sighed with her usual drama queen finesse. "I didn't ask you to cover for me, so don't go acting like I owe you anything."

A gust of her breath hit him—she smelled like a brewery. "You were out *drinking?* On a *school* night?"

His voice sounded ridiculously shrill and parental even to him, and Aimee actually started to laugh.

"Bite me, Shane." She brushed past him, her full lips pressed into a line. "You live your life and I'll live mine, okay? Just get out of my face."

"Come on, Aimee!" He could feel his blood pressure surge and clenched his hands into fists. She could be so unbelievably selfish. "Dad's going to catch on sooner or later, even if I keep making up stories. He's not an idiot. He's got to be wondering what you're up to, out so late all the time. I can't believe you're pulling this crap all over again."

"Pulling what?!" She whipped her head around. "I have a life, Shane. Or at least I'm trying to have one."

Before he could say another word, she was storming out of the house.

Aimee stalked along the path leading to the woods behind their house, moving at a fast clip. Shane sounded like an old woman, coming down on her like that. *Who the hell does he think he is?* she thought. *What I do is none of his goddamn business.*

But she knew that wasn't true. It was his business because he was just trying to watch out for their father. And as she walked and the cold air cooled her temper, she was willing to admit he could be right. But Shane's words *hurt*. He was acting like she was some kind of drunken slut and implying that maybe her dad thought that way too. Some of the losers up in Boston had talked to her that way, but she didn't expect it from her brother.

To this day she had no idea who had started spreading the garbage about her, but even remembering the things she'd heard were written on the walls in the boys' room at her old school was enough to make her want to curl up and die. Aimee liked to flirt, she liked to dance, and she liked an occasional drink, but that didn't make her a slut.

Aimee blinked back the sting in her eyes. No way in hell was she going to give Shane the satisfaction of making her cry. It wasn't going to happen.

She walked along the path through the woods that bordered their side of the street. Maybe half an acre into the trees, far enough that she could pretend she was alone and get away from everything, there was a large flat rock just right for sitting on that was calling her name. She'd found it the day after they came to Sleepy Hollow. It was her secret place and right now she needed to be alone.

So, naturally, her brother followed her. She heard him stomping through the woods after her and calling her name, and she didn't want to deal with him. Sometimes he could be such a complete idiot.

"Stop following me, Shane! I mean it!"

"Aimee, look, I was out of line. . . ."

"I swear if I hear anything like that around the school, I'll beat you to death!"

"What? Aimee, come on, you know I'd never say anything like that!"

"And don't go thinking you walk on water, Shane!

You think Dad's worried about me? Well, news flash, big brother, he's just as worried about you!"

He snorted a half laugh. "I'm not the one going out every night."

"No, you're the one who never goes out. You're the one most likely to climb a tall building with a sharp-shooter's rifle."

"What?"

"You heard me. Shane, you didn't even cry at Mom's funeral, you never do anything but stay locked away in your room, and the closest thing you've had to a real emotion in the last year was getting off on a really tasty slice of pizza!"

This time it was Shane who looked confused, and that gave Aimee a little burst of triumph. She was getting tired of his holier-than-thou attitude. "At least I have something resembling a social life," she continued, on a roll. "You don't think Dad worries about you lurking around in your room? He's probably worried you're going to start building bombs to take out the school!"

"At least if I'm at home when I'm supposed to be, he doesn't have to worry about me getting cut to pieces." Shane's face was red, angry. That suited her just fine. Aimee was in the mood for a knock-down, drag-out fight.

And she might have done something about it, might have moved in for the verbal kill and started on a few of the rumors that had been spread about him in

Boston, if he hadn't suddenly gone deathly white and looked past her.

Aimee closed her mouth and listened.

And heard the slow steady sound of hoofbeats coming in their direction from deeper in the woods. There was no hurry to the sounds. The horse was walking, not running. But the clomp, clomp, clomp of those hooves was enough to make the fine hairs on the back of her neck stand on end. Aimee's eyes widened as she looked to her big brother.

Maybe twenty yards away, she heard the sound of a horse whickering impatiently. And then the hooves pounded into the ground as the horse charged.

Aimee took just long enough to look, to see the horse and rider moving through the trees in their direction, and then her hand sought and found Shane's and the two of them took off.

They dodged around the trees, the sound of thunder cutting the ground behind them as the black beast and its rider came closer. Shane cursed and suddenly yanked Aimee completely off her feet so that she lurched backward as the horse and rider cut in front of them, literally where Aimee would have been standing if her brother hadn't intervened.

The horse turned sharply and she watched the ground being cut into shreds by its iron-shod hooves. When Aimee was ten, her mom and dad had treated her and Shane to a day of horseback riding for her birthday.

None of the animals they'd seen at the Rocking W Horse Farm had been anywhere near as large as the shadowy stallion. Every step the beast took fairly shook the ground.

Shane reached down and grabbed a rock about the size of a softball, looking back toward the horseman as he came back around for another charge. The rider held himself low over the horse. He reached to his side and swept his right arm into the air, brandishing a sword that gleamed darkly in the light of the moon.

Aimee stared at that blade, transfixed, her mind playing back the head of Henry Mickle rolling to a stop between her ankles. *That's the blade, the sword he used to cut off that poor man's head. . . .*

Shane pushed her roughly, almost knocking her off her feet, and screamed for her to move. The horseman's weapon cut a screaming path over her head, missing by mere inches. Aimee dropped low and rolled, moving out of the way.

Her brother wasn't quite so lucky. One of the stallion's flanks slammed into him and he was thrown through the air, landing in the thick mulch. Shane gasped like a fish trying to breathe air and got back to his feet, the rock he carried clenched in a death grip.

Aimee ran his way, conscious of the rider pulling the reins, the night black horse rearing up and turning around again, ready to finish them both even if it had to use its hooves. Shane pitched the rock as hard as he could, grunting with the effort, even as he started running again. The rider took his hand off the bridle and reached, snatching the missile from the air. And as he did so, he moved into a wide shaft of moonlight streaming down through the branches above and the siblings got their first steady look at him.

The dark green jacket, filigreed with gold thread, showed clearly in the moonlight, as did the black breeches, the black leather riding boots with cuffs folded down, and the thick leather riding gloves that could just as easily have been used by a falconer. The gray cloak around his shoulders billowed but didn't hide the fact that there was only a stump where his head should have been. The wound there looked fresh, the skin raw and red and the bone and muscles gleaming wetly.

Aimee froze completely and Shane only stood beside her, stunned by the sight of the Headless Horseman. The legend of Sleepy Hollow. With a casual flick of his wrist, the rider tossed the rock back toward Shane, who managed to dodge it by mere inches, the wind whistling off the projectile. The rock hit a gnarled old oak behind them and broke thick bark away.

Then horse and rider charged again, moving toward them with relentless fury. Aimee shrieked. Shane shouted in alarm, grabbing at her, but she knew that it was already too late, that they were about to die. Aimee closed her eyes, terrified, wishing she'd done more with her life.

The horse jumped, lifted into the air above them,

thick hooves dropping sod on their shoulders as the steed shot past, landing behind them with unsettling grace and then weaving between the trees at a fast gallop.

A moment later the woods were silent around them. Aimee and Shane looked at each other, eyes wide, faces pale, gasping for breath.

They ran like hell all the way home. The Horseman had been toying with them. Playing a game. Aimee knew that, knew it with the same conviction that let her know her own name.

But why?

Cassie Winthorpe sat up in bed, breathing hard, her sleep shattered by the sound of her front door slamming with enough force to rattle the windows. She'd been having the nicest dream about being back in college and dating Johnny Depp, but that was blown away by the sudden noise.

Richard. The thought sent icicles down her spine. She shivered, rolling her tongue back to the hole in her teeth where her ex-husband had knocked out a molar in their last fight. She reached down beside her bed and picked up the butcher knife she'd taken to keeping nearby and stood up, her knees trembling with fear that he was in the house.

Down the hallway she heard the sound of glass breaking, a fine sharp tinkle followed by a lot of smaller ones and a heavy thudding crash that told her the credenza where she kept her knickknacks had just fallen over. The credenza that weighed in at around three hundred pounds.

She reached for the phone and dialed 911. Cassie wasn't a coward, but she wasn't a fool either. She'd kicked Richard out when he got too mean and she'd called the cops on him when he left. She called them again now because for all she knew, Richard was back in town and ready to once again try to explain how the world was supposed to work in the house he called a home.

The ringing of the phone on the other end seemed to last forever, and Cassie gripped her knife harder, ready to cut Richard's heart out if she had to. He'd certainly done a number on hers over the years, and fair was fair. She giggled nervously, trying to come to terms with the gallows humor she felt bubbling through her mind. She'd never been so scared in her entire life.

Cassie crept to the door as someone finally answered the phone. She rested the small headset against her shoulder and opened the door carefully, ready to slam it shut in an instant if she had to. The doors were heavy oak these days, replacing the flimsy plywood that had been there before Richard went berserk and tried to beat her to death. He could try to kick his way through, but it would take a mule to put a dent in the wood.

Or maybe a deer? Even as the voice on the other end of the line asked her about the nature of her emergency, Cassie heard the rhythmic clop of an animal walking on the hardwood floor outside her room. She almost laughed, relief flooding her. "I think I have an animal in my house," she said. She took her hand off the doorknob and breathed deeply, her pulse pounding in her skull. "Oh God! I thought it was my ex-husband coming back to kill me."

The crystal doorknob turned, light fracturing on each facet.

Cassie's eyes grew wide and she let out a gasp as the door opened.

She only managed half a scream. The second half was cut off, along with her head, as the blade slammed through the phone cord and her neck.

"WE'RE OKAY, DAD," Shane said. "Seriously. We're all right."

"Look. We're in one piece." Aimee gave a weak smile. "Well, two pieces. Me, one, and him, one."

Their father didn't smile. He was beyond smiling. His hands gripped the steering wheel so tight that his knuckles were white and he shook his head every few seconds. His face was flushed.

"We moved here to get away from . . ." Alan frowned. "It's supposed to be safe here. Quiet."

"It *is* quiet." Aimee was in the backseat, hugging herself, her eyes still wide and her face still pale, maybe in a little shock over what they'd seen.

No. Not maybe. Definitely. Shane was still reeling as well. And now they had Dad's reaction to deal with.

"But nowhere is completely safe," Aimee added.

Their father shot her an angry look before putting his focus on the road again. That head-shaking thing continued.

"I promised your mother I'd keep you safe. That I'd give

you a good life." He was barely talking to them now. "What do I do about this? A little town like Sleepy Hollow, and I've got to worry about murder? About some lunatic chasing after my kids, pretending he's the Headless Horseman?"

Shane felt the words coming to his lips and knew he shouldn't speak them. Aimee did it for him.

"I don't think he was pretending," she said.

Alan had been on edge since picking them up. Now he whipped around in the car, hitting the brake. "What are you talking about? Aimee, don't get thoughts like that in your head. The Headless Horseman, he's just a legend in a story. People don't keep walking around if someone's cut their—"

Aimee flinched. Shane felt his stomach flip-flop.

Their father paled and seemed to deflate. "I'm sorry. God, that . . . I can't believe you had to go through that." He turned forward in his seat and accelerated again. "I wish I could just erase it from your minds."

"So do I," Aimee whispered.

Shane swallowed. "Aimee's telling the truth," he said.

Alan knitted his brow and glanced at Shane. He shook his head again, but this was a different sort of denial. There was desperation in his eyes. He was so afraid for them, so shattered by the thought of what might have happened to them, but so far he'd only been dealing with their physical safety. The way he looked at Shane then, it was obvious he was thinking about their mental well-being now too.

"Shane. It's not possible. You know that. You're more practical than that."

"It's what we saw." He shrugged, not wanting to push it, knowing his father was having a hard enough time already with this. But people had to know that it was real.

"What you thought you saw, maybe," his father said softly, in that way people talked to small children and lunatics. "But it was dark, Shane, and you said yourself it happened fast."

"You could see the stump of his neck!" Aimee said, voice cracking, hugging herself tightly.

"No." Alan shook his head. "A costume, Aimee. Some kind of getup to help with the illusion. A freak, taking advantage of the local legends for effect. Someone murdered Mr. Mickle, and that's a terrible thing. But the killer is just a twisted, dangerous man. The police will find him, and then you'll see."

A change passed over his face then, and some of his fear for them was replaced by other concerns. "Keep it simple when we talk to Chief Burroughs." He raised a hand to stop any further argument. "The fact that you were attacked by someone dressed as the Headless Horseman is enough, okay?"

Aimee and Stasia sat in the living room, watching MTV. It was the first even remotely relaxing time Aimee'd spent all day.

"I heard this rumor that they used to actually show

music videos on this channel," Stasia said, a smirk on her face.

"Seriously?" Aimee asked. "Weird."

She had told Stasia everything, including what had happened with the Horseman and their visit to the police station. Chief Burroughs had been quick to chalk it up to some freak or even a prank, suggesting it might be someone's idea of a sick joke and not even the same person who'd killed Mr. Mickle.

"But you saw what you saw," Stasia had said.

Aimee had only nodded.

"What about the fight you and Shane had?" Stasia sounded worried, which was sweet of her.

"We're okay, I guess. We agreed not to talk to Dad about any more of this stuff, though. The . . . you know, the weird stuff. He doesn't believe us anyway, so what's the point?"

"Where is Shane?" Stasia frowned, looking around as if half expecting him to come along and ruin everything.

"You can relax. He's at the library, reading up on the legend of Sleepy Hollow and the Headless Horseman. I don't know how he can even go back into that building."

"I've got the book. He could read my copy."

"Not that sort of research. He's trying to find out more about Washington Irving and what made him write the story in the first place. And about what the town was like back in those days."

"So you and Shane, you really think it was the Headless Horseman?"

Aimee shivered and glanced away for a moment, the image of the Horseman still fresh in her mind. She hugged herself. "I know it sounds impossible," she said quietly. "I wouldn't believe it myself if you told me. But I saw him. I'm not messing with your head on that. It wasn't a costume. I could see the . . . I could see the neck bones where they'd been cut. Seriously."

Stasia looked away from her for a second and then looked back. Her eyes were wider than usual and she gnawed at her lower lip nervously. "You promise not to laugh if I tell you something?"

"Huh? Of course I won't laugh." Aimee frowned. "I just told you I was chased by a headless guy. Where would I have room to laugh at you?"

"I think my house is haunted."

Aimee flinched, heart skipping a beat. "Excuse me?"

"I think my house is haunted. I haven't seen anything, but Aimee, I'm scared to go home at night."

"Then how do you know it's haunted?"

"Look, you know I've always been into this stuff. Like a hobby. There've been rumors that my house was haunted for generations; that's why I started looking into all the occult stuff, so I could maybe get lucky enough to see a ghost someday or know if I got visited." Stasia looked intently at Aimee, like she was trying to see if her friend was going to rag on her. "I mean,

I know what the signs are, at least according to most of the books, and I've heard them and felt them, but I've never seen them."

"Like what?"

"Like cold spots, okay? My room is like a refrigerator sometimes, and late at night? I hear whispers. I know it's not my parents. They're working at the restaurant a lot of times. I can be all alone in the house and I hear this little voice whispering in the next room or I hear footsteps going down the halls. And one time I thought I saw something, but it was so fast I figured it was just my imagination."

Stasia's face, normally so old for her age, looked like a little kid's and Aimee felt for her. "So let's find out what's causing it."

"Really?" The relief in Stasia's voice was obvious.

"Absolutely." Then she thought about it a moment. With all that had happened, she was pretty sure Shane didn't doubt the existence of spooky stuff like Hizzoner anymore. Or the whispering tree. They'd seen the Horseman. Instead of needing someone to prove these things were true, at this point Aimee figured they were both convinced enough to need someone to prove they *weren't*. And if there were ghosts . . .

"Let me call Shane and we can have him come along. He could probably use a break from the books anyway."

Stasia nodded enthusiastically, clearly grateful for the help. Aimee smiled and squeezed her friend's hand for a second before dialing Shane's cell phone.

CHAPTER
EIGHT

THE TRAEGER HOUSE was a large colonial with a low stone wall all the way around it and matching stones around its base. It was old; Shane could tell that much immediately, though architecture was hardly his strong suit.

"So, your family's disgustingly rich?" He cast an eye on Stasia, soaking in her low-rise jeans, her light gray shirt, and the thick, rich curls of her hair.

She smiled. "No, just lucky. My dad's family has lived in the same place since Sleepy Hollow was established."

"Seriously?"

"Yep. Come on in, I'll give you guys the two-dollar tour, free of charge this once."

They entered the house through the front door and almost immediately ran across a tall man with a long face and receding hairline. He made up for the bald spot with a beard and mustache. He walked toward them with a wide grin on his open, friendly face.

"Hi, Pop." Stasia gave her father a one-armed hug,

but he quickly picked her up like a little kid and squeezed her in a bear hug.

Shane was taken aback for a second. After all the times Stasia'd done all she could to avoid going home, he'd pretty much come to the conclusion that her parents might just be ogres. Not the case, at least as far as her father was concerned.

"Good to see you, honey," he said as he gently dropped her back down. "I feel like I haven't seen you in weeks."

"Well, I'm not the one always hanging around in bars late at night." Her voice had a teasing tone.

"I'm not hanging around in bars; I just steal wine from them for cooking." It seemed like one of those conversations they'd had a hundred times before. Shane decided he liked Stasia's father.

"This is my friend Aimee and her brother, Shane. They moved to Sleepy Hollow just a few weeks ago."

"Well, any friend of Stasia's is a friend of mine. You kids want something to eat? Maybe something to drink?" Mr. Traeger shook both of their hands with the enthusiasm of a used-car salesman and then stepped back to let them enter the living room.

Aimee and Shane looked around, impressed with the place. It was comfortable and well laid out. The sofa looked like it could seat about ten with ease.

"Oh, no. You are not fattening up my friends. Not tonight, anyway." Stasia grinned. "We've got to look up a few things real quick. Maybe after."

"Well, if you guys don't have plans for dinner, I have some leftovers from work I can heat up."

"Um . . ." Stasia looked at the two of them.

Her father seemed to genuinely want to impress his daughter's friends, so Shane figured no harm. Their dad was going to be working late again anyway. He did a quick check with Aimee and then nodded.

"Okay. But don't pull out the big guns, Dad. I need them both able to walk," Stasia joked.

A few moments later they were on the stairs heading for Stasia's room. "My dad has a tendency to over-feed people," she said. "He thinks the best way to handle any situation from war to watching TV is to lay out a gourmet meal."

Even as they climbed to the second story, they could hear Mr. Traeger starting in on the kitchen with enough noise to rattle the windows.

Stasia's room had a lived-in quality, though for the most part it wasn't messy. Shane did see her make a hasty run at the closet and watched, amused, as she shoved some underwear into a laundry basket near the closet door. The bed was a queen-size affair with all the decorations he was used to seeing in his sister's room—lace around the sides, lace around the bottom, the whole nine yards. The only thing missing was Aimee's collection of stuffed animals. Still, even without the stuffed animals, he was surprised that Stasia had such a girly bed. Just one more intriguing thing about her to add to the list—despite appearances, she really did have a softer side to her.

He forced his eyes away from the bed, doing his best to shut out all the associated images that poured into his mind. To the left of the bed was an old rolltop desk that had to be an antique, and next to that was a stereo system that would have made most of the kids he knew in Boston absolutely green with envy. Next to the closet where Stasia stood was a bookshelf loaded down with books of every shape and size and with only one real theme. Shane grinned like a kid at Christmas and ran over to look.

"*Tolliver's Myths, The Compendium of Apparitions, Ghosts and Goblins, Crowley's Compendium of Exotic Botanicals, A Study of the Supernatural,* by Michael Wagner . . ." He read the titles with a slight hint of awe. Some of the books were obviously newer editions, but a few of them looked almost as old as the house. "Stasia, these are great!"

Stasia looked like a proud mother. "Aren't they?" She ran her fingers lightly over the spines, and Shane looked over the titles again. There were books in the collection that he knew had to be worth hundreds of dollars. "My grandmother used to read these kinds of books too, so I got lucky. Some of these are impossible to find."

Aimee let out an exasperated sigh and Shane looked over at his sister with one raised eyebrow. She was apparently already bored with the idea of anything that could have to do with books. Stasia was *her* friend, so he got the hint and let the two of them talk for a few minutes, listening as Aimee started asking questions about the ghost and the experiences Stasia had been through. And while he listened, he looked around the bedroom. There was a pair of underwear at the foot of the bed that she'd missed in the laundry sweep. Where had she found underwear with pink skulls?

Stasia was explaining in detail where every encounter with the ghostly presence had taken place, and Shane focused on that instead. It was less complicated. She gave them the tour, and when they'd gone over the place pretty well, she looked disappointed. "Nothing. Not even a cold spot. It's like the stupid ghost is hiding."

They were standing in the hallway outside her room when the temperature dropped around them. "Whoa! You feel that?" Shane whispered.

Even if they hadn't felt it, the two girls could see it as the breath of his words fogged heavily. Aimee's jaw dropped open, and he realized his own had as well. Shane ran his hands through the air, trying to get a rough idea of how big the spot was. But before he could really imagine the dimensions, the sudden chill faded away.

"Damn. It's like it was making sure we believed you." He looked at Stasia as he spoke and she nodded, blinking quickly. He'd seen that sort of expression before, on Miss America contestants when they finally calmed down enough to give acceptance speeches. It was happiness, relief, and a little amazement.

"I think it did." She jumped up and down on her toes, the most emotion she'd ever displayed around him. "I really think it did, Shane!"

After that, they went downstairs to dig into the "leftovers" Stasia's dad had set up for them—a gourmet meal that would have probably cost them a hundred dollars a plate in Boston.

As they ate, they got down to business. "I think we need to do more research," Shane said. "I'm going to try the Hall of Records and see what I can find out about your house."

Aimee nodded. "That's your territory. I think Stasia and I better go see what we can find out about Hizzoner."

"The dog?" Shane scrunched his eyebrows together. "Why?"

"Well," Stasia spoke up. "Everything started happening around the same time—Hizzoner, the Horseman, all the other weird stuff around town. I kind of doubt that's a coincidence."

"So maybe it's all connected?" Shane ventured. "The Horseman and the dog and all the other weird crap going down?" Obviously he could see why that would be the logical assumption, but it sort of rubbed against his nature to assume the random events were connected just because that was the easy answer. After all, they were still missing the nice, rational *reason* behind these things.

"Think about it, Shane," Aimee said. "Everything

in town suddenly goes crazy and you don't think there's a connection?"

He shrugged. "Just because some of this stuff is true . . ." He paused. "Which is still just . . . just nuts. But even if some of it is true, that doesn't mean all of it is. I mean, some of the people we've seen, locals getting themselves on TV or calling in to the paper about, you know, mermaids or whatever—they're so obviously crazy."

Stasia's expression was heartbreakingly sincere. "Have you ever heard the expression, 'Just because you're paranoid doesn't mean they're not out to get you'? Well, just because they're crazy, that doesn't mean the things they're seeing aren't really there."

"Okay." Shane paused. "So, what are you going to do? Go out to where Hizzoner is supposed to hang around?"

"No, Shane. We thought we'd start getting interviews from people on the street." Aimee rolled her eyes at Stasia. "Of course that's what we'll do."

Stasia nodded. "If I can figure out if it's a spirit or an animal, I might have something that can stop it from hurting anyone."

"Like what?"

"Some of the books in my room cover protection from certain types of spirits. I don't know if they really work, but there's only one way to find out." She grinned so broadly he thought her face would split. "I've only been waiting my whole life for a chance to see if any of that stuff actually works."

Shane shifted uneasily. "But what makes us ghost-busters all of a sudden? I mean, as far as I'm concerned, we've already been a little too close to this as it is."

"Look," Aimee said, "for some reason, we seem to be the only people who get what could really be going on here. And if all of this stuff really is connected, then we need to know that to put all the pieces of this puzzle together. And let's face it, brother of mine. Nobody can put together a puzzle like you can."

Stasia arched an eyebrow. "I've heard that about you."

He met her gaze for a second, then looked away. "Fine, I guess you're right. But you two be careful." Crap. There he went, sounding like his father again. "Bad enough the police are probably looking for scapegoats instead of the real thing, but if there is any truth to Hizzoner, I don't want to have to try gluing you back together."

Half an hour after eating, Shane was on the move, walking toward the library several blocks down. Who would have thought going back *there* would ever have felt like a relief? But amazingly, right now even the site of that nightmare was better than being in Stasia's home, looking at her across the table, thinking all kinds of thoughts he really couldn't be thinking.

As he walked, several police cars—state troopers this time, not the police department—shot past him. When he got close to the building, he heard and then saw a helicopter moving overhead. A bright spotlight from the aircraft cut through the darkness, searching the ground in the distance. He had no idea if it was a police copter or a news crew and was even less certain when he saw the news vans that blocked half of the library's small parking lot.

There were two vans that he could see, and both of them had spilled out complete crews, who were trying to make reports over the sound of the helicopter and the police cars that were in the area, apparently just to make sure the news crews behaved themselves appropriately. As he walked past the Warner Public Library's front doors, he saw an old man, probably in his sixties, being interviewed. The man's short white hair was perfectly in place, and his slightly too old suit was pressed, but he looked positively frantic.

Shane felt a ripple of fear. Was all of this craziness still over Mr. Mickle's murder? Or had someone else been . . . ? No, Sleepy Hollow was a small town, and the press had been attacking this story with a vengeance. He was sure this was just more of the same craziness his dad had been complaining about—widespread panic and attention that wasn't helping to solve the crime at all.

Two of the Sleepy Hollow Police Department's finest were looking Shane's way. He'd seen them before, but unlike in times past, they didn't exactly look relaxed. One of them, a tall lean man with short black hair and a caterpillar mustache under his nose, walked his way, frowning. "Shouldn't you be at home, son?"

Son? If the cop was ten years older than he was, Shane would have been surprised. "I was just heading that way, Officer . . ." He looked at the man's badge and name tag. "Officer Dunfee."

"Make sure you do, son."

The other officer, a few years older but not any heavier, walked up and put a hand on Dunfee's shoulder. His badge said his name was Murphy. "Ease up, Tommy. This is Alan Lancaster's boy."

"What? The newspaper guy?"

"Yes. The new editor for the *Gazette*. He probably already knows what's going on."

"Shane?"

Shane turned his head fast at the sound of his father's voice. "What are you doing out here alone?"

"What, Dad? I'm sixteen."

Alan grabbed Shane's arm lightly, directing him past the two police officers. "Come on, I'll give you a lift."

"Dad, it's only a few blocks."

"I don't care. I don't want you out after dark by yourself." His expression was grave. "There's been a second murder."

Shane blinked at the confirmation of the fear he hadn't even allowed himself to form in his thoughts just moments ago. "A second . . . Who? When?"

Alan shook his head. "That's not important right now. What matters is that if it was the killer who chased you . . . we have to be careful. With this second murder people are really going crazy. See that man? The one being interviewed?" Shane nodded. "That's Harry Shannon. He used to be a teacher at your school. He's gone on a crusade, calling the press and telling them that we have two decapitation murders and that the Headless Horseman is responsible."

"But we already—"

"I don't want to hear about what you saw right now; you just listen." Shane would have taken more offense at his father's tone if he hadn't seen the worry lines on his dad's face. "There's a panic starting and I don't want you or Aimee caught up in it. Half the stores closed early and a lot of the restaurants are thinking about doing the same thing. That old man isn't doing anyone any favors spreading his legend stuff around, and the press from down in Manhattan are doing their best to make this a media event. And he isn't alone. A lot of senior citizens out there are swearing that it's the legend come to life and out to slay anything moving."

Alan urged Shane into the car and then climbed in himself before continuing. "Trust me, Shane. The crazies are going to come out of the woodwork here. And more importantly, there's a *real* killer out here somewhere, and he might believe you and Aimee got a good look at him. I don't want you on the street. I'm taking you home and I want you to stay there, understand?"

"Okay, Dad."

"Where's Aimee?"

"She's over at Stasia's, staying the night." The lie was fast and off the cuff. He didn't want his dad worrying himself into an ulcer over Aimee. "I walked her over and then I was going to the library to work on this new paper I have in English."

"Well, tonight you get to do your research on the Internet. I don't want you out." He pulled into the driveway of their house. The lights were all off and the place looked about as cheerful as a mausoleum in the darkness. "Chief Burroughs is considering a curfew, but there won't be any decisions made by the town council until tomorrow morning."

Shane sighed. Some things never changed. His dad wanted to avoid a panic in the town, but he was already close to panic himself at the thought that his children might be out in the dark.

Shane climbed out of the car. Alan followed suit, but not to go up to the house. He just wanted to make sure his son was paying attention to him. "I mean it, Shane. Promise me you won't go anywhere tonight."

"I promise, Dad." He shrugged. "I don't have anywhere to go. The library's closed." The look his father cast his way was unreadable in the near darkness, but finally the man nodded and climbed back into his car.

A moment later Shane was alone, and not long after that he was inside and heading toward his bedroom and computer. He decided to start at the very beginning and looked up Washington Irving online. Once he'd found what he was looking for, he settled in and began to read "The Legend of Sleepy Hollow," Irving's most famous work.

"Think we should have brought dog biscuits, just in case?" Aimee asked.

Stasia smiled thinly but didn't respond until she'd set down the supplies they'd gathered. "I don't think a Scooby Snack is going to calm down Hizzoner. From what I've heard, he's out for blood."

Aimee hugged herself and rubbed her arms. It was chillier than she had expected. "Okay, so we know ghosts are real and the Headless Horseman is real." She still had a hard time saying such things out loud, and even mentioning the Horseman gave her waking nightmares. "Couldn't we just accept that the dog is real and not be here?"

"No way. Besides, we have stuff to fight back with."

"Look, Stasia, no offense, but I don't really trust sticks and flowers to keep a ghost from eating my face." She paced a bit, looking at the supplies Stasia laid out on the ground not far from the road. Long grass and a few scraggly bushes partly hid them, but if Burroughs drove by, there would be a lot of explaining to do.

Stasia's hands deftly separated the branches she'd collected. "Birch, rowan, holly, four small apples, red ribbon . . . Give me the bag, Aimee."

Aimee set down the plastic bag they'd brought along. Inside it was a jar filled with golden liquid and two pairs of disposable latex gloves.

"Thanks. Start tying everything together in bundles, okay? One of each branch, like I have them here." She gestured and Aimee squatted next to her. Stasia's fingers wound a red ribbon over and between the branches in what looked like a rather complicated pattern. But after Stasia showed her, it wasn't that difficult to duplicate, just time consuming.

"Okay, so if this works, will it drive the ghost out of your house?"

"No. Hizzoner isn't a ghost. Not really. He's a black dog."

"What's the difference?"

"Well, black dogs are supposed to be 'harbingers of doom.' That means they're supposed to show up and give warnings of danger."

Okay, so there wasn't a whole lot of logic going into the idea of stopping the dog thingie. It was scaring the crap out of people but maybe not intent on hurting anyone. Still, it would be interesting to see if anything happened. Aimee wasn't exactly expecting much. The cold spot in Stasia's house might mean something freaky, and the Horseman was—she shuddered just thinking of him. But Hizzoner was less likely to be real as far as she was concerned. "So he's not going to eat us if he catches us here?"

"Well, I didn't say all they did was give warnings. A lot of them seem to like killing people."

"Oh, yeah, that helps." Aimee nodded dramatically. "That's a great way of warning people. Makes sense."

"According to the legend, Hizzoner is supposed to be looking for his master. Maybe he's trying to find whoever killed his master and is just a little confused."

"So apples on a stick will help with this how?"

"They're called wards. If we do this right and place one at each corner of the crossroads, it's supposed to prevent the black dog from being able to manifest. And, you know, eat everyone."

Aimee smiled halfheartedly. "Oh. It's all good, then."

They'd already gone over the basics. Aimee even knew that the liquid part of the jar was cat urine. Gross. She hadn't asked how Stasia had gotten the pee and didn't want to know. She was grateful, however, for the rubber gloves. Once everything was set, they were supposed to soak the bundles in cat urine and then place them in the right spots. There was some sort of chant that Stasia had to say and then everything would be all right. If it worked, which, of course, they couldn't know until they were done.

Something rustled in the distance, and Aimee paused, her hands going cold. But she didn't hear anything else and reminded herself that there were plenty of *normal* animals out there in the bushes. No need to freak out.

Stasia took a collection of twigs and a poultice wrapped in an old stocking and set it down. "That's one." She poured a little of the urine over the bundle and grimaced. Her hands were bare.

"What happened with the gloves?"

"I figured I'll wear them when I have to tie these in place."

"Where do you tie them?"

"At each of the four corners of the crossroads." She took a bundle from Aimee and saturated it. "Then I have to say the magic words and it's supposed to be—"

She was cut off by the sound of something heavy moving through the long grass not far from where they crouched in the darkness. Aimee looked at Stasia. "I think we might have company."

Stasia held up her hand and cocked her head, then waited. When nothing else happened, she moved across the street as quickly and quietly as anyone Aimee had ever seen and started tying one of her bundles to the branch of a tree. If Aimee hadn't actually been watching, she'd have never spotted the ward.

Stasia came back, repeated the procedure again, and urged Aimee to finish the last two bundles. She'd just started when Stasia came back a second time. "Okay. Two more and then I can say what I'm supposed to and maybe we can find out if this is going to work." Stasia sounded nervous, which was unusual in and of itself, and Aimee's heart skipped a beat.

"What's wrong?" she asked.

"That noise you heard?"

"Yeah?"

"I'm thinking maybe it's something we should worry about."

"Like . . ." Aimee didn't want to say it. Didn't want to think it.

"Hello? Really big black dog?"

That was when the growling started. It came from somewhere off to the right, near a few old oaks on the side of the road. Aimee looked in the direction of the noise and felt her heart start pounding away for real now.

At first it was nothing but a large black lump in the darkness. Then it growled again and she saw fangs glistening yellow in the moonlight. *The better to eat you with, my dear,* she thought. Then she saw the eyes, red as blood and glowing above that razor smile.

Stasia's scream was louder. Aimee's was swifter.

Unfortunately, the black dog was faster than either one of them.

CHAPTER
NINE

THE SOUND OF the grass being mashed down by her feet was loud but nothing next to the deep roar that came from the thing behind her. Aimee risked a look over her shoulder and saw Stasia right on her heels, eyes wide and limbs moving at high speed. She was gaining fast, at least.

Hizzoner was gaining faster. The dog couldn't be natural. There just wasn't any way. It was as big as a grizzly, with fangs and claws and burning eyes. And she could feel the hate and the hunger coming off it like the wind off the ocean and a blast of heat like she'd just opened a furnace and looked inside. *Is this what evil feels like?*

Aimee's breath was ragged in her throat and her legs were barely keeping up with her body. It felt like any second her momentum would take over and she would break her stride, trip over her own legs, and go sprawling.

They'd almost made it to the blacktop, not that far, really, when Aimee saw headlights farther up the road and coming nearer. She ran toward them, a prayer in her heart that came out of her mouth as another scream. Then the blue flashers on top of the cruiser cut the night open in a lightning strobe of blue.

Chief Ed Burroughs pulled the cruiser to the side of the road and stepped out of the car, looking at the two girls expectantly. Aimee looked over her shoulder and saw Stasia doing the same. There was nothing but darkness behind her. No sign of Hizzoner.

"What the hell are you doing out here, Miss Lancaster?" Even from ten yards off, the man sounded annoyed. "Do you really think it's a good idea to be out here at night?"

"No, sir, but—"

"Now, I know your father's already been chewing on your brother for being out alone tonight. Had a couple of boys tell me all about that one. What makes you think he's going to take it any better if he finds out you're hanging around where there's supposed to be a vicious animal on the prowl?" Burroughs moved closer as he spoke, his face set in the sort of scowl that made people worry before they tried anything stupid.

"We were just seeing if there was any truth to the stories."

"And did you find anything?" His eyes cut from Aimee to Stasia and back again, his face keeping that expression that said he'd just swallowed something he didn't much like the taste of.

"Yes! We just saw—"

118

"No, Officer Burroughs, we didn't." Stasia stepped forward. "There was a lot of noise and it sounded like a big dog, but we chickened out and ran. That's when you saw us."

The words flowed easily past Stasia's lips, and her eyes locked with the chief's. Aimee looked back at her, stunned, but didn't counter her words.

"Well, that should tell you something, shouldn't it?" He moved closer, taking each of the girls by an arm. "That should tell you that there's nothing here but a bunch of nervous people and maybe a stray mutt. Now you've had your fun and it's time for me to take you home. There might not be a curfew officially yet, but you two are getting one anyway. Personalized service from the chief. Be honored."

Both girls were wise enough to keep their mouths shut. He put them in the back of his cruiser, where the doors didn't open on their own. Where they kept the terminally stupid who had to go to jail.

Aimee was glad to see that he drove toward Stasia's house. They had too much to talk about and she wasn't planning on going home.

"Listen, girls, I really mean it. Be careful. There's a murderer out there."

He pulled the cruiser into the driveway of Stasia's house, killing the headlights just before he drove up the hill leading to her front door. Once there he stepped out of the car and opened the door for the girls. As soon as he'd pulled away, Stasia flipped a one-finger salute at the cruiser.

"He thinks we're both trouble," she said.

Aimee nodded. "Well, he's right."

"He's a hardass, but he was at the right place tonight." Stasia's voice was soft, but there was a gleam in her eyes. Aimee was still so numb with terror and relief, she couldn't believe Stasia was actually excited by what they'd just seen.

"He's real, Stasia. The black dog." It came out in one breath and Aimee shook her head. "I thought like any second I was going to feel those teeth on me. . . ."

Stasia nodded. "Yeah. He got there too fast. We didn't finish the wards."

"I almost wish he'd let himself get seen by Burroughs."

"He let himself get seen by us. That's enough." Stasia moved closer and put a hand on Aimee's shoulder. "Now we know he's real."

"So now we have a ghost, a demon dog, and a Headless Horseman. What else is real around here that shouldn't be?"

Stasia started toward the house, pulling Aimee along. "I don't know. But I can't wait to find out."

Aimee and Shane said their goodbyes to Jekyll and Hyde and moved toward the cafeteria. Aimee had filled Shane in during biology, between watching Steve's usual antics and listening to the murmurs about a possible curfew. Remarkably little actual class work got done. Even Ms. Dimitrios had apparently given up on getting anything accomplished. She'd just handed out mimeographed work sheets and glared around the room for the next fifty minutes.

Curfew. It was an ugly, ugly word. Not as unattractive as *beheaded,* or *murdered,* or *chased-through-the-woods-by-a-psycho-with-a-sword,* but still ugly.

Stasia was waiting for them at a corner table when they got there. She'd packed her own lunch, which was far more appetizing than what was served by the cafeteria staff. Cardboard pizza wasn't horrible, really, but for some reason they'd served it with mashed potatoes and green beans.

They didn't bother much with idle chitchat. Instead they got down to the business of their plans for the afternoon and evening.

"I'm going by Town Hall," Shane said. "I need to finish looking over those papers I was searching for the other day. I found them just before they were closing. So now that I know where to look, I have to actually do the digging."

"Have you seen the *Gazette* yet?" Stasia asked. Her eyes were the most amazing color. . . .

"Um. No." He coughed. "But I was thinking I'd go there after Town Hall and see if I can look up some of the archives. I don't know what they're going to have—I mean, we're talking about really old papers, and you just know they haven't been scanned into a hard drive anywhere. But if they have a microfiche, I'll check into it."

"They do," she assured him. "I've looked up a few things in the past. You can't even touch the original papers, I don't think, but they copied them all."

God, she was amazing. He realized he'd forgotten Aimee was even there. It was like he and Stasia were alone. The very thought of which made his face flush. What would he say to Stasia if they were *actually* alone together?

"I've been thinking," Aimee began.

"Uh-oh," Shane and Stasia said in unison.

Aimee shot them a withering glare. "Excuse me, but hey! There will be none of you two ganging up on me ever, or blood will flow."

"Check," Stasia said, nodding.

Shane flashed a quick, totally fake smile, then looked down at his tray, unable to meet either of their gazes.

"Anyway," Aimee said, "I'm thinking maybe Stasia and I should start looking for the whispering tree. You know, since it's probably connected to everything else too."

Shane frowned. "You think that's smart?"

"Probably not." His sister wiped at imaginary pizza stains around her mouth with a napkin. "But it's a tree, right? So we go see it in the daytime and find out if there's anything to the stories."

"Okay, but what if it tries to do something?"

"Did you miss the part where it's a tree?" She sipped her milk. "What's it going to do? We'll be there in the daylight and we'll stay away from it. All we want to do is see if it really does foretell the future or give out secrets. Because if it does, it might be able to help us solve the problems we're running up against."

Stasia reached out and touched Shane's arm, her blue eyes looking into his. He pretty much had to look back, if only so it didn't seem like she affected him. "I think Aimee's right. Call it intuition or just paranoia." She laughed softly and he held his breath.

"But it's a *tree*," he argued.

"Shane," Stasia said, squeezing his arm. "We've been over this already. You've read a lot of the same books I have. If black dogs are real, and ghosts . . . think about how many other stories there are, how many myths and legends."

He nodded slowly, the reality of that sinking in with a gnawing dread. "I'm not sure I want to."

"Anyway, we're going after school. You look into the paperwork, and we'll do the field testing." Aimee spoke dismissively, like it was already a done thing. Maybe to her it was.

"Okay. What do we do if you find this tree? We can't very well run to Dad or the cops, can we?"

"God, no," Stasia said. "We already know they won't believe us. We could drag the Horseman in front of them and they'd just try to explain it as a costume where someone did a great job of hiding the zipper."

Aimee pushed her empty lunch tray back and stretched her arms over her head. "We find out what these things are and what they want. Maybe then we can get enough information to make even Dad see reason. Or enough to let the police figure out how to fix the problem." She shrugged. "Right now we just find out what the tree is. Later we can work out how to handle it."

"I just . . ." Shane trailed off. "I know I've already said this, but we're dealing with serious stuff here. Two people are dead." He lowered his voice even further, narrowing his eyes. "Even if it's all supernatural—and yeah, Stasia, I find that almost as exciting as you do—it's still dangerous. Maybe even more dangerous than some ordinary idiot with a knife. It's . . . it's nightmare stuff, you guys. I'd be lying if I said it didn't scare the hell out of me."

Aimee opened her mouth, looking like she was about to snap a typical retort. Then her expression softened and she looked away. "All right. True enough. I don't ever want to see that dog again." She lifted her eyes and stared at him. "But Shane, if the police aren't even willing to consider the things we saw, the things we know are true, how are they ever going to be able to stop the Horseman? Who knows how many people he'll kill? If we can't convince them, then I think the only choice is for the people who really know and believe what's happening to figure out how to stop him, or . . . or banish him, or whatever you do with . . ."

She glanced at Stasia for help.

"Demonic manifestations?" Stasia suggested with a small shrug.

"Whatever," Aimee said, returning her attention to Shane. "I'm not saying I ever want to see the Horseman again. But if we can figure out why he's here, maybe we can get rid of him without having to."

Shane sighed. He felt pretty stupid being more frightened than his little sister. But he was also terrified enough to get over that feeling if it meant staying alive and never having to see that night black horse or hear its hooves pounding the earth again.

What sucked was, Aimee was right.

"Okay."

Aimee nodded in approval, as if for once she thought her brother might be pretty cool. She stood up and Stasia did as well, her chair scraping the floor as she pushed it back.

"My hero," Stasia said, and she bent and quickly kissed the top of his head.

Aimee laughed softly.

Shane, on the other hand, couldn't figure out how to respond. A thousand fragmentary thoughts went through his mind. He wondered if either of the girls would be able to interpret the look on his face and hoped not.

"Call me when you're done looking for the tree," he said quickly, trying to hide his emotions. "I need to know where you are if I'm going to cover for you with Dad."

"Will do," Aimee said.

Then they were gone. Shane's last words echoed in his own mind. Here he was, lying to his dad to cover for her again. They were doing something important, not just out partying at all hours and starting trouble. But it didn't make him feel any better.

"Okay. It's a cornfield." Aimee tried to make herself sound brave even as she looked around nervously. She was from Boston, and she was used to feeling a little claustrophobic in tight areas, where buildings towered and the crowds of people and cars were enough to make you feel like everything was hedging you in. But the corn was creepy, even with the sun shining above. The wind moved the stalks, and they whispered and moved and knocked against each other with the faintest rattles. Stasia had wanted to stop here on their way into the woods to look for the tree because of what Derek had said happened to him. But right now Aimee was feeling more than ready to move on.

"No. I think there might really be something here." Stasia spoke calmly but softly, too. Like she was afraid to be heard too clearly. "I can feel it, can't you? But I don't think it likes the daylight too much." She looked at the corn growing in the fields around the Ingalsby farm and frowned. "I think it's hiding."

"Well, either way, I don't think there's much we can do about seeing it in the daylight, and we still need to find that tree before the sun sets. And I feel silly just standing here and waiting for something to happen."

"You're right," Stasia agreed with a sigh. "We should get started looking for the tree before it gets any later."

So they went, moving into the woods at the edge of the farm, where the land rose up toward the hills that overlooked the rest of the town. It was the Hudson River Valley, after all, and the whole town was a slope from the highest hill all the way down to the bank of the river. Stasia seemed to know the woods well, which was a big plus in Aimee's eyes because after almost an hour of wandering through thicker and thicker forest, she was thoroughly lost.

Meanwhile, they hadn't found anything strange. All the trees were just that. She had no idea what she had expected—maybe angry, talking trees that threw their own fruit, like in *The Wizard of Oz*. They stopped to rest in a small clearing. Autumn wasn't in full swing, but already the ground was covered with fallen leaves.

The discussion had moved to boys, which was no real surprise. But what *did* surprise Aimee was what Stasia had to say about Mark Hyde and Steve Delisle. "It's not like either of them is my type," Stasia began. She perched on a moss-covered boulder. "I mean, Jekyll's seriously hyperactive, and when he's not in overdrive, he's stoned. And Hyde . . . he's a little too intense. But still, they're each kind of cute in their own offbeat way, you know?"

Aimee was trying to decide how to react to that

particular revelation when they heard the whispers. Stasia cocked her head and listened, and Aimee strained to hear where the sounds came from. The voice, low and insinuating, issued from a tree just behind her.

At first glance there was nothing remarkable about it. It looked like an old oak, complete with gnarled branches and a deep, pitted knothole a few feet off the ground. It wasn't a beautiful tree, nor was it majestic, but it was big. The branches were thick and strong and the roots were half buried, with several thrusting from the ground like long fingers grasping at the soil.

But looking a second time, really paying attention, Aimee thought something was *wrong* about it. The sun was beginning its descent, and most of the trees were now in a hazy sort of shade, but this one tree seemed to stand in a deeper pocket of eclipse, as if it created its own shadows to compete with the ones around it. The knothole seemed almost the source of all the cold bleakness that enveloped the tree.

Aimee started to back away, but before she had taken the first step, she heard the whispers more clearly than before.

The whispering tree called her name. *Aimeeeeee. Open your heart. Listen well.* She froze, transfixed. Her breath caught in her throat and her eyes widened. She wanted to shake her head in denial, but the voice was there, right inside her head, and it would not be denied. The words seemed to come to her as the rustle of leaves, hissed secrets that were shared with her by the wind. Foolishly she listened.

Shane doesn't trust you. Not like he should, not like you trust him. She blinked, feeling that the words were true without really knowing why. *Your mother hated the sight of you toward the end. She hated your vitality and wanted to steal it from you.*

"No," she murmured.

The wind stung her eyes and made them water. There could be no truth to those words; her mother had loved her. Yet there had been times when her mother's pretty face had seemed drawn with lines of bitter regret. Maybe there was a little seed of truth in the words after all. She tore her gaze from the tree just for a moment and saw Stasia shaking her head. The other girl was mouthing something, some response, and she understood then that the tree was in Stasia's head too but that she was hearing other truths, her own unwelcome secrets.

The world seemed to warp around Aimee. In the back of her mind she knew she had to get away, to flee this thing, and she tried to force her limbs to obey that urge. But she was frozen with the words. The whispers. And a terror that rose in her heart. She did not want to hear what the tree had to say, even if it was the truth. Especially if it was the truth. *Your father suspects what happens when he is not home. He's smelled the beer on your breath. He thinks you are a whore. You frighten him.*

"S-Shut up. You're lying." The wind kept stinging

her eyes. She was sure that was why the tears started falling. It couldn't have been the words the tree made worm their way into her head, because that would mean that everything she was hearing was true.

Was that laughter she heard from the tree or merely the rustle and creak of branches pushed by the harsh winds? She couldn't tell. *John Devon was the one who said you were easy. He told everyone that you practically begged him to have sex with you. He started it, but Kyle Wilson and Brett Chambers helped him spread the word.*

That was a gut punch. Aimee took a deep breath and tried to think because John Devon was one of her friends, one of the guys she had trusted in Boston, and that he could have been the one who started the rumors hurt more than she wanted to admit. If it was true, she'd never trust a guy again.

You think Stasia is your friend. But she has used you to get close to your brother. When you need her, she will not be there to help you.

Aimee winced, the words like knives. As she listened, lost in the secrets and the whispers, the sun began to set. And the tree came for her.

CHAPTER
TEN

AIMEE TRIED TO make herself move, tried to run from the dark secrets the tree shared. They couldn't be true. At least . . . they couldn't *all* be true. Friends and family alike were not what she expected, hoped they would be, and the world around her seemed like it wanted nothing more than to crush her beneath a tide of misery.

She heard herself whimper, felt her teeth biting into the soft flesh of her lower lip, and shook her head as the skin broke and hot blood ran across her tongue. Maybe it was the sudden lance of pain in her lip or the tears in her eyes or simply the sickening feeling of being violated in her heart and soul, but she finally managed to move.

Aimee stumbled, her legs weak, and fell on her back in the damp leaves around the whispering tree. She shivered more than the chill evening air could account for and blinked rapidly, disoriented.

"Stasia?" Her voice sounded winded, strained, and she made herself gasp in a deep breath. "Stasia?"

Her friend didn't answer. Aimee looked around and

tried to shake the echoing cobwebs of dark thoughts from her head—*She has used you. . . . When you need her, she will not be there to help you*—only partially succeeding. But when she saw Stasia, her thoughts became clearer.

Aimee had been much closer to the tree than Stasia. Now, though, Stasia wasn't near the tree, but on it. Her body was completely off the ground, a thick branch wrapped halfway around her waist. Even as Aimee caught sight of this horrible scene, the wood creaked and the branch tightened and lifted Stasia off the ground. Something thick and black slithered from the depths of the big knothole in the tree's bark, dripping a heavy, foul-smelling sap as it slid up Stasia's ankle. It curled around her calf, pulling her foot toward the darkness in the gaping maw of a knothole. The black pit had grown; Aimee was sure of it. She had no trouble believing her friend's entire body could be pulled into the thing with little effort.

Stasia's eyelids fluttered as if she were drugged and she made soft whimpering noises. Her face was streaked with tears, her lips trembling.

It had lulled them somehow, and now the tree was going to kill Stasia. *When you need her, she will not be there to help you.* There was no way in hell that Aimee was going to let anything happen to her friend.

"Let go of her!" The words burst from her lips in a scream that scraped her throat raw. Aimee ran to Stasia, her fingers grabbed at the bark, and she nearly pulled away, disgusted to feel that it was warm and damp. The rough bark tried to catch her skin, to cut into her fingers. She pulled as hard as she could on the branch that held Stasia, throwing her weight into the struggle, but all she got were a friction burn on her fingers and a slight swaying of the limb.

With a grunt of effort she braced her feet against the tree, pulling hard even as the black serpentine thing that had caressed Stasia's ankle whipped around and wrapped around Aimee's own leg at the knee.

The breeze became a howl of fury and the tree shuddered, fighting against her as she pulled and strained, her muscles feeling like they would pop away from her bones and her head pounding with the effort. Tears burned her eyes. Her chest tightened so much she couldn't breathe. Her body trembled with fear and adrenaline.

And then the branch cracked, splitting along one side, splintering as strips of bark and wood popped away in a deep V. Aimee fell, hitting the ground, and Stasia fell with her, landing half on top of her.

Stasia let out a ragged sigh and pulled in a deep breath, her eyes flying wide as she looked around. Aimee kicked and screamed, the slimy tongue of wet black still clenching her leg. She felt herself lifted and pulled, drawn toward the knothole, and went a little crazy. She kicked, she clawed, she shrieked and bucked wildly, the heel of her free foot pounding down into the pulpy wet mass that held her tightly.

133

And then she was free, falling a second time and pushing back from the tree with desperate speed. Stasia looked at her and then finally stood up, moving away from the tree herself, her eyes still wide, gleaming.

The oak tree shivered, the one broken limb waving as if caught by a hurricane, and thick red sap spilled across the ground near Aimee's feet. She grabbed Stasia's arm and ran, pulling her friend along until a hundred yards separated them from the tree.

Aimee panted, terrified. Stasia looked back at the tree, barely visible past the foliage of other trees and bushes. And then Stasia laughed openly and loudly.

"What the hell is so funny?" Aimee demanded, her throat raw, her heart still thundering. "That thing almost ate us alive!"

Stasia looked at her, her cheeks bright with excitement. "Don't you get it? I mean, I believed before, but in the back of my mind I knew the Horseman could have been a hoax. And the black dog—we saw it, but it could have been some animal bred like that. And the ghost . . . I felt the cold but don't have any proof, only my *feelings*." She pointed at the tree. "This, baby, this is proof!"

"I get that, but why are you laughing?"

Stasia sobered a bit, but she still had that kid-on-Christmas-morning grin pasted to her face. "Aimee, all my life I wanted to know there's more than just—" She waved her hands around, encompassing the entire area.

"More than just the stupid news on TV and the crap we have to learn in school. I wanted to know that there's magic in the world. And now I do. For sure."

"Well, go watch David Blaine!" Aimee shivered. "You almost died just now!"

Stasia moved over to her and hugged her hard. "I know. And thank you for saving me." Aimee looked back at the tree, almost swallowed by darkness now, and shivered again, grateful for the human contact.

"It said things to me, Stasia. Did it talk to you?"

"Yeah. It did. It told me all sorts of stuff that I didn't want to hear." Stasia reached down and touched the skin where the tree's black tongue had gripped her leg. "It said my mom was . . . unfaithful to my dad last year." The flesh looked swollen and angry, like a patch of poison-ivy-coated skin. "I thought that she was out a lot, and I know the two of them haven't really been close in a while. They try to take different shifts at the restaurant; they're almost never home at the same time if they can help it." Her face got stony. "That thing is evil." Her voice was soft, barely above a whisper.

Aimee shuddered again, remembering what it had said about Stasia using her to get close to Shane. But she shook it off. The tree had to have sensed something in her, traces of her anger at Shane for the last time he hooked up with a friend of hers and how ugly that had gotten. The idea that Stasia and Shane . . . It was ridiculous. She sighed and gazed at Stasia.

"You have something we can kill that with in your books?"

"I don't know. I never ran across anything like that. At least I don't think I did. Besides, it's not like I'm a witch, Aimee. All I have is what's written in the folklore to protect against different things."

"Well, I'm new to this, Stasia. I'm sort of looking to you as the expert here." Her words came out harsher than she meant and she winced, apologizing with her eyes.

"We'll look, okay?" Stasia said, flashing a smile to show she wasn't mad. "Maybe we can find something."

"If we don't, I'm coming back out here with a gallon of gas and a blowtorch."

Stasia nodded. "I'll help." They walked in silence for a minute, and then Stasia asked the question Aimee had been dreading. "What did the tree say to you?"

Aimee swallowed and told her, leaving out only—*when you need her, she will not be there to help you*—what the tree had said about Stasia.

She was just getting to the end of the revelations when Stasia looked at her watch. "Oh, crap!"

"What—it's around five, right?"

"Try almost six-thirty."

"What?" Aimee's voice rose. "That's impossible!"

"I don't think so, Aimee. I thought it was just the woods, you know, but I don't see the sun anywhere."

"My dad's going to kill me." Aimee was trying to be better, at least when her dad was at home, about being on time. Especially since the murders. She felt a flash of guilt even as she thought about it. That damned tree was messing with her even now.

Stasia stopped. "I don't think that's going to be a problem."

"What? Why?" She'd been lost in her own thoughts and Stasia's comment confused her at first. Then she heard the deep clomp of a horse's hoof thudding into the ground and heard the gust of breath as the animal moved closer.

"Run, Stasia! *Run!*"

Both girls bolted, and as soon as they moved, the Horseman exploded from the deeper woods behind them, moving fast, the steed beneath him charging after them. Low branches lashed at their legs and Stasia let out small gasps of pain between breaths. The Headless Horseman wove between the trees, never coming too close but never leaving them a chance to stop and rest.

Just do it, you bastard, Aimee thought. *If you're going to kill us, just do it.* The way he toyed with them was torment.

The girls ran. The muscles in Aimee's side twisted up in a stitch that stung deeply, but she didn't slow down. The Horseman was relentless, pursuing them past obstacles that should have slowed the horse. Worse still, he was steadily gaining.

When Aimee caught sight of the low post-and-beam fence that marked the back edge of the Traegers' property, she was torn between relief and a dreadful certainty that now the game would end, that he would give them this moment of hope and then eviscerate them. Both of them were sweating, gasping for breath as they vaulted the fence. Aimee risked a glance over her shoulder and stumbled to a halt. Stasia noticed that she had stopped and turned to see what had happened.

The Horseman sat on his mount, unmoving, gloved hands tight on the reins. Even though he didn't have a head, it still felt like he was staring at them. Watching them. Then he bolted back up the hill into the deeper part of the woods.

Shane rubbed his eyes, desperate to get rid of the grit that had them burning. The sun had set and he was still searching through records at the town hall. He should have left hours ago, but he'd gotten deeply engrossed in the documents he'd found the other day, so he had hidden himself away in a corner when the lady who ran the place came to tell him he had to go. He'd noticed earlier that the rear doors locked automatically, and he figured he could slip out when he was done without leaving the place unsecured.

Now he had gotten all the information he could from the town's records. He had made monumental leaps in what he suspected, but he wasn't much farther along in concrete facts. It was infuriating how many gaps there were in the documents he'd looked through. He'd started by digging deep into the archives, seeking information on the Headless Horseman. That was a dead end, but he'd found things that were even more interesting to him.

For instance, the fact that Ichabod Crane wasn't a fictional character after all. He was a real person who had lived in Sleepy Hollow and had been the subject of a lot of controversy for the town council. The reports about their council meetings were full of references to Crane, to promises he had made to them and to their concern that he was endangering the town. Most of these records were buried deep in boxes that hadn't been moved in at least a few decades. They were meticulous about details of day-to-day life in Sleepy Hollow, but every time the subject of Crane came up, pages would be missing. In some cases sections had been cut out, and in others the bound copies of these meeting reports had pages where someone had blacked out words by brushing a layer of ink over them . . . sometimes over the entire page. Despite his best efforts to look at the words under the ink, they had been too thorough.

Somebody wanted every word that had been written on the controversy surrounding Ichabod Crane eradicated. Shane's eyes burned from sorting through the papers, lifting layers of dust that were probably older than he was into the air. He'd been going nonstop for better than five hours and that was after a day of school. But he wasn't tired. He was anxious. Something big had been hidden in those old journals and notes. He just had to figure out what it was.

He had no proof of anything, not really, but he thought he might know how to get it. One place might hold some answers: the archives of the *Gazette*.

The Headless Horseman was real. Shane had seen it with his own eyes. So Washington Irving clearly hadn't made him up. But now it seemed Ichabod Crane had been real too, which meant "The Legend of Sleepy Hollow" was a lot more fact than fiction. He'd also turned up evidence that Washington Irving had lived in Sleepy Hollow, at least for a while. Still, from what he'd seen, Irving had made lots of changes to whatever the *real* deal was with the Horseman and Crane, because the truth didn't seem to be what he'd written in that story. Irving had probably played around with the elements to suit his needs as a storyteller. Or . . . because there was another reason he couldn't reveal the truth.

Shane squinted at the papers in front of him, searching for details that would bring this all into focus. He scanned the names in the ledgers and books and minutes of various town meetings and suddenly got a curious rush. They were names he knew from street signs and from people in town. There was even a Van Brunt, which was where Derek came into the equation, a Van Tassel, and a few others.

But that didn't explain what the Horseman was doing back in the hollow now or what whoever had blacked out these old records had been trying to hide.

It was time to go see his father at the newspaper

and maybe do a little more digging. He stretched and his back and neck popped. Then he looked down at his watch and groaned.

"Damn! It's after eight." He stood up and carefully started putting the old documents back where they belonged; he might break an occasional rule, but he wasn't about to make someone else clean up the mess. He worked quickly and had everything where it belonged in short order.

His book bag over his shoulder, he slipped out the back door of the building. A minute later he was on Broadway and walking toward the paper. His stomach fluttered a few times as he realized he was outside in the dark alone. He'd told his father he would be more careful. Well, his father would be at the paper if today was like every other day since they'd moved to town, and he could explain when he got there.

The stores were all closed. A couple of blocks away he saw one car drive down the street. That was it. He could have been living in a postapocalyptic nightmare world for all the people he was seeing. In a town with over nine thousand people, that was a little weird.

Shane moved faster. It was only a few blocks to the paper and relative safety.

The clip-clop of hooves on pavement echoed off the faces of darkened buildings.

Shane turned, already knowing what he would see. The Horseman sat atop his steed, regal and deadly.

Where there should have been a head, there was nothing but air. A streetlight flickered behind him—the only one that had been replaced on the entire stretch of road.

Shane dropped the heavy book bag down into his right hand. The collar on the Horseman's cloak twitched and somehow it looked like he was nodding his approval. Shane bit back hysterical laughter and gripped the shoulder straps on the bag harder.

Simple physics in action: a twenty-pound sack of paper hurts just as much as a twenty-pound rock when it slams into the chest of a moving object. The Headless Horseman knew what Shane was doing. Somehow he'd seen it without eyes and understood that Shane had a weapon. So he'd nodded his approval, and now to make sure Shane understood too, he drew his long sword with a whistle of metal against metal. He held the blade before him, metal gleaming in the single streetlight, sword raised in a mockingly formal salute.

And then he charged. Maybe twenty yards separated Shane from the horse and rider. Instinct overrode courage and terror both. Book bag still in hand, he ran as hard as he could, his shoes slapping the ground lightly as a counterpoint to the sound of iron-shod hooves pounding asphalt. The Horseman rode up on him, then came up right beside him, and there was nowhere for Shane to go. The stores and restaurants to his left were closed, their doors tantalizingly close but locked. He could shatter a window, but if he managed to get inside, he'd only be cutting off any route for his own escape. The road ahead offered no shelter, and to the right the massive horse paced him so close that he could see the fine hairs on the beast's hide.

The horse bumped him and the ground was gone from beneath his feet and he was rolling over and over and over across the asphalt. He felt the bag escape his grasp and rocket away from him as he tumbled. He came to a stop on his back and looked up at the darkened sky. The moon was far above him, a pale ghost behind clouds that obscured all but the faintest light. Then the silhouette of the Horseman blocked even that. Hooves clacked against the ground, slower than before.

The figure lifted something heavy and tossed it at Shane. For one second he just knew a bloody, decapitated head was going to land in his lap and he let out a panicked gasp. A weight slammed into his stomach and Shane sat up, breathless, and tried to stand. The horseman backed away on his stallion, the sword still in his right hand.

Shane looked down to see his book bag on the ground. Not a head, just his books. His feeble weapon against the nightmare before him.

The horse and rider wheeled suddenly and rode hard, cutting through the darkness, then disappearing up a side street. Shane looked after them for a few moments and then glanced around at where he was. The doors to the *Sleepy Hollow Gazette* were only a few feet away. He took an uncertain step forward, trying to regain command over his shaking legs. Step, deep breath. Step, deep breath. By the time he made it to the newspaper office, he was actually walking without having to make the conscious, concerted effort to move his limbs.

The only person in the office was Professor Bisby, the arts and entertainment writer with the bad bow tie fetish. He was at a desk, typing something on the computer.

"Um, hi." Shane's voice had a recognizable edge to it, and he paused, licking his lips. "Is my dad here?"

"No, Shane, he isn't." Bisby frowned. "He's at home. The town council pushed the curfew through. You're not even supposed to be outside your house right now." His expression softened. "You look like you've been running a marathon. Is everything okay?"

"Yeah." He nodded. "I just lost track of the time and thought I'd see if my dad was here, let him know I'm okay."

"Well, he's probably worried sick. You might want to give him a call."

"I will, thanks." Bisby went about whatever he was doing after curfew for the newspaper and Shane dialed home. His father answered on the second ring.

"Hi, Dad."

"Shane! Where the hell are you? You're supposed to be here right now."

"I know, Dad. I'm sorry. I was studying and lost track of the time. I didn't think it was this late. When I saw the time, I came over to the *Gazette* to give you a call."

"You just stay there, Shane. I'll be right over."

"Is Aimee home yet?"

"No. She's staying at Stasia's again." He could hear the disapproval in his father's voice. "She just called about an hour ago herself. You know, I gave you kids cell phones so this sort of thing wouldn't happen."

"I'll try to remember to carry it, Dad. It's just not something I usually think about." It was stupid, obviously, not to have the phone with him, considering he knew even better than his dad just how much danger was really out there. But what would a cell phone actually do anyway if the Horseman finally decided to stop toying with him and take him down? It wasn't like making a quick phone call would be much help.

"Okay. Just wait there. I'm on my way, all right?"

"I'm not going anywhere."

"Good. And tell the professor to wrap things up— the article can wait. There's no reason for him to get a fine for breaking curfew."

Shane nodded into the phone. "Will do."

He disconnected the call, then passed along the message to Professor Bisby. As Shane sat in the front office to wait, he tried to get his pulse to slow down to normal speed. It wasn't easy. He picked up the phone again and dug into his wallet for Stasia's phone number. She answered on the fourth ring.

"Hi, Stasia. It's Shane. Can I talk to Aimee?"

"Oh, yeah, hang on."

After another minute Aimee answered. "What's up, bro?" Her voice was too carefree, too light.

"I had a little run-in a few minutes ago. With *him*. Did you find what you were looking for?"

"Yeah. Yeah, we did. It's the real deal. And . . . he came after us, too." Her voice was a whisper. He suspected that with the curfew, Stasia's parents were probably home.

"I don't understand," Shane said, glancing over to see if Bisby was paying any attention to him. But Bisby's gaze was locked on his screen. "I mean, he could get us anytime he wants to. Why is he playing around like this?"

"I wish I knew. But . . . I'm thinking it's better than the alternative."

"Oh, yeah." Shane winced. "Listen, can you meet me at Washington Irving's house tomorrow?"

"What? Why?"

"I want to look into something and I might need your help. Can you do it?"

"I don't even know where his house is, Shane."

He gave her the address. "Just meet me, okay?" He listened to her breathing. "We can go over everything then. Right now I have Dad coming to pick me up."

"Okay. Around one?"

"That's perfect. I could use the chance to actually sleep in a bit." The weekend was more than welcome at this point—it was pretty hard focusing on anything at school.

"See you then."

He hung up the phone and settled in to wait. Every

shadow that went by in front of the building made him jump. Though it had started to grow on him, Shane hadn't really wanted to move to Sleepy Hollow in the first place.

It seemed the feeling was mutual.

The parking lot was empty when Harry Shannon pulled up, and that was just fine. He wanted to get in, get out, and be on his way without being noticed by anyone. He killed the engine on the old station wagon and shivered.

There was so much to do and so little time. The stress of the last few days was making him nervous and he didn't want to be out here in the night, when almost anything could happen.

Out of the station wagon and moving fast for the building, he was ready to grab and run before anything could get him. He shoved the car keys into his jacket automatically, reassured by the jingle they made as the weight settled in. In and out. That was the plan and he was sticking to it. At least he meant to.

The sound of hooves clacking against the asphalt made him freeze. They weren't soft, casual sounds. The hooves struck the ground in a rapid tattoo and Harry Shannon turned to see the dark figure of a man with no head bearing down on him.

"Oh God. No, not yet. Please! I can make it better. Just give me a chance to find it!"

The hellish apparition thundered toward him. The retired schoolteacher turned and tried to make it back into his car, his hand already digging in his jacket pocket for his keys.

Fingers clenched around the small key ring and he pulled it into the open air.

A sharp whistling sound reached his ears just before he felt the bite of steel against the back of his neck.

CHAPTER
ELEVEN

AIMEE PACED BACK and forth impatiently. A Manhattan news crew was parked near Washington Irving's house, looking for people to interview. Aimee didn't want to be their target, so she waited for Shane across the street. A female reporter with delusions of youth was trying to look perky and to sound sincere. She was failing.

Bored, Aimee wandered over to a newspaper box and put in two quarters to get out a copy of the *Gazette*. She wanted to see what her father had to say about what was going on and how he was handling the entire thing. The headline was direct and to the point:

THIRD VICTIM FOUND BEHEADED

She scanned the article and then moved to a few related ones. The police chief was offering ideas about what sort of maniac would use an old legend to frighten people. An editorial by her father urged that everyone remain calm and ignore the attention from the national media. He warned against going out at night and breaking the curfew, but he also cautioned people to remember that the killer was only human and that he would eventually be captured.

Aimee glanced up from the paper from time to time. Eventually the news crew went on their way. She started across the street and felt an almost overwhelming wave of relief wash through her when she saw Shane coming around the corner of the house. Aimee ran instead of walking and hugged her brother tightly. He looked a little taken aback but then returned the hug just as strongly.

"I'm glad you're in one piece," she said, flushing a bit at the admission.

He grinned. "The feeling's mutual."

For just a moment the things the tree had said about Stasia and Shane flashed across her mind, but Aimee brushed them off. They'd all been hunted last night, and she was just happy he was all right. And anyway, he and Stasia had hardly spoken to each other except at the lunch table until all this weird crap had started.

"You all right?" Shane asked.

Aimee nodded, pushing her thoughts away. "Yeah. Just . . . the tree really messed with our heads, trying to get us to doubt everything and everyone. It lulls you that way, distracts you until it can attack. Trust me. Not fun."

Shane scuffed his foot on the sidewalk. "Well, like what? What'd it say?"

She regarded him for a moment. Most of what the

tree had said was too personal, too hurtful to repeat regardless of whether she believed it. But . . . "All kinds of crazy things. To make me think Dad hates me or—"

"Dad doesn't hate you; that's ridiculous."

She waved his protest away. "I know. Seriously. I mean, there was also this thing about you and Stasia, like there was something going on with you two. Crazy, right?"

For just a moment Shane's eyes widened and Aimee wasn't sure what he was going to say. Then he smirked. "I barely know her. Somehow I don't think a girl like Stasia's gonna be interested in your boring brother."

Aimee grinned. "See, that's what *I'm* saying."

Shane rolled his eyes and smiled sheepishly. After they'd caught up on the previous night's encounters, he led her around the side of the house. "I think I'm starting to understand what's going on, but I can't find any solid proof."

"What did you find out?" Her heart beat a little faster.

"Nothing concrete yet. But I think I'm on to something." Shane looked around, his eyes bleary and bloodshot. "It's what I'm not finding. You get me? It's what I'm not seeing and what I should be seeing that keeps eating at me."

Aimee took a deep breath and nodded. She had to remind herself to be calm. "Okay. Start from the beginning, Shane. What are you talking about?"

"All right. I went to look at the papers at the town hall. I looked over everything I could find there about

Washington Irving and about his life and when he lived here especially." He started pacing in the front yard of the Irving house. "I figured maybe there was something to what he wrote, you know? But maybe there was something that he *didn't* write, too."

Aimee looked around. The area was pretty much deserted, but she didn't feel comfortable just standing out in the open. She moved to the side of the old house and Shane followed.

"Anyway." He waved his arms distractedly. "At first I found references about him moving to the area and not much after that. But there was more, Aimee. I wasn't really looking for Irving; I was looking for proof that the Headless Horseman existed. Maybe a mention or two of something back then, a murderer who worked the same way. Anything like that."

"Okay. I'm with you. What did you find?"

"Ichabod Crane."

Aimee felt a weird, sickening twist in her stomach. "But Ichabod Crane was just a character in the story."

"So was the Horseman. Or not. The Horseman's real and so was Ichabod. Now here's the bizarre stuff. I found only a couple of places where they used his full name. Everywhere else he was just I. C. There were all kinds of town council records, meetings where they talked about him."

"Wow." She swallowed. "So the whole story was real."

"Maybe. And maybe not." He was doing it again,

talking in circles. "I think the story is just a little bit of the whole picture."

"You're confusing the hell out of me, Shane."

"There was more to it than what Irving wrote."

Aimee studied him. "Like what?"

"That's what I'm getting to—I don't know. Because whole sections of the meeting records are either ripped out or blotted out with black ink. Like someone wanted to erase a whole piece of this town's history. And everywhere you find that stuff, it's always connected to some record of a conversation about 'I. C.' Sometimes even with him having been at the meetings."

"What are they trying to hide?" she wondered aloud.

"That's the big question. I even went back to Dad's offices and did a microfiche search, and I found exactly the same thing. A whole lot of nothing. Someone cut a bunch of stories out of those old newspapers. Whatever they were trying to hide . . . I think it was something like what's happening now. All kinds of weirdness. And all somehow connected to Ichabod Crane. I think there were all sorts of freaky things going down in town back then, and I think they hid them. Somebody didn't want anyone to know that there were monsters in Sleepy Hollow."

"Okay, but why?"

"That's the part I'm not sure about yet. There had to be a reason, but I don't know what it was."

"Maybe it wasn't monsters, Shane. Maybe it was just crimes or a witch trial or something." She paced in a tight circle, a lump in her throat. Shane was normally the calm and rational one, and he was clearly agitated. "They could have just been hiding something that they did to someone who was innocent or something."

"No. They didn't have any problem reporting crimes. There're plenty of records showing when someone did something wrong and what happened to them. But Aimee, they even marked out obituaries, like they didn't want to admit that some people lived in Sleepy Hollow at all. Or that certain people died here. Like the Horseman's victims way back when."

"Okay, Shane. I get it. Big-time mystery and maybe you're right. Maybe it's all connected. But if you hit a dead end, why do you seem so excited about it?"

"It wasn't a total dead end," he said, his face intense. "I found out something about the Horseman's victims. His latest victims." Shane seemed to finally manage to get his thoughts in order. It was like watching a switch get flipped.

"Shane, spill it."

"I was looking up everything I could about the founding of Sleepy Hollow and the people who lived here back then. I was trying to find out how much truth there was in Irving's story. I found a pattern."

Shane reached into his pocket and pulled out a folded sheet of notebook paper. "It's all here, Aimee. Names from back then and names from now. Take a look."

Aimee looked at the paper. There were two columns

of names scrawled in Shane's barely legible handwriting. On the left-hand side was a list of seven names all under a date that ran back over two hundred years. Some of the names were oddly familiar, and some meant nothing: Harold Shannon, Walter Mickle, Jedediah Winthorpe, Theodore Hasselbeck, Adam DeMarchant, and two more where Shane's usual messy handwriting was too sloppy for her to read. Below that list were a few more that had been kept separate: Washington Irving, Abraham Van Brunt, Hendrick Hudson, Ichabod Crane, Katrina Van Tassel, and Baltus Van Tassel. On the right-hand side of the paper was a much shorter list: Henry Mickle and Cassie Winthorpe. She recognized both names, of course. As if she could ever forget Henry Mickle's. She shivered as she stared at the names of the two victims of the Headless Horseman.

"Wait, why do you have Harry Shannon on the nineteenth-century side?"

"That isn't Harry Shannon. It's Harold Shannon, his ancestor, who was a member of the town council when Sleepy Hollow was founded."

"You're kidding." But she knew he wasn't. She looked over the names again. If Shane was right, it was obvious what the Horseman was doing. He was hunting the descendants of the men who had been on the town council the last time he had ridden this land, when Ichabod Crane had lived in the hollow. That meant Harry Shannon and some other locals were in serious danger.

155

"I have one other thing to show you." He grabbed her hand and pulled her gently away from the street, toward the back of the small cottage. "This way." Shane spoke as he walked, his voice oddly subdued. "There's a list of names on the bottom of the page, where you see *Washington Irving* written. See it?" She nodded and he continued. "That list is names from the story."

"Okay. What about it?"

"The names seemed . . . familiar. I wrote down the ones that I thought might be important. Like Van Brunt. Only in the story it was Abraham, or Brom for short—not Derek. We know Washington Irving lived in this house, but did you ever wonder why he chose it over any of the others in town? It wasn't just because it was the only empty house; at least I don't think so." He crouched low when they reached the corner of the house and pointed to a spot near the ground that was overgrown with weeds. "Guess who lived in this house before him."

Aimee sighed and squatted next to her brother, looking and not seeing anything. "It's a corner. Wow, you found a dark secret here."

"Sarcasm? You're not seeing it, Aimee. Look closer." He brushed a few of the weeds aside and pointed to the lowest brick in the wall. Aimee stared for a few seconds before she saw what he was indicating. On the lowest stone, carved in thin letters: *I. C.*

Aimee blew out a long breath. Shane had found it in the records, but seeing it like that, engraved in stone, made it real in a way that even the Horseman wasn't. He'd tried to kill her and her brother—or at least to terrify them—but he was some kind of supernatural thing, some force they couldn't control any more than they could the weather. A force of nature. But that stone was real. Just as real as the man who had engraved those letters there.

"Ichabod Crane," Aimee whispered.

"If any part of the story really is true, he lived here and was chased away or killed by the Headless Horseman."

"We have to tell Dad, Shane. We have to let him know."

"Yeah, we do. And the chief too."

Aimee looked around one last time and nodded. "Let's get it done and then get home. I don't want to be out after dark."

The sun was heading west as they walked to the offices of the *Gazette*. Aimee was shivering with the chill of early autumn—but she knew it wasn't just the cold.

Shane walked quickly. Aimee hurried to keep up. They entered the building and nodded to Eunice, the elderly woman behind the desk. Their father was in his office, looking as frazzled as Aimee felt. Before Shane could open his mouth, Aimee jumped in with a recap of what Shane had discovered. She knew her brother wanted to do it himself, but he just took too long to explain things.

Alan Lancaster scanned the single sheet of paper Shane handed him and then inhaled deeply before raising his gaze back to his children. "What made you start looking into this?" he asked, focusing a hard look on Shane.

Eunice appeared in the open doorway, but their father didn't take his eyes away from Shane's.

Shane never blinked. He just shot the lie out of his mouth. "I'm doing research for a paper on Washington Irving, and I decided to look at the town records. I sort of caught the name connections."

Aimee watched her father's face closely, worried about whether or not he'd buy Shane's explanation.

Eunice cleared her throat politely. "Actually, Shane, the library has a selection of Washington Irving's personal letters and journals. They might be a good source for information, certainly better than the town's records. Those are a mess. Alan, I've got Ed Burroughs on line two. I think you'll want to talk to him."

Without bothering to wait for a response, she vanished back into the main office.

Alan held up a hand to let them know to stay put, then answered the phone. "Hi, Ed. What's on your mind?"

Aimee looked at her father and watched his face pale, his eyes widen. He looked around his desk and then realized he still held Shane's list in his hand. He flipped the page up so he could read the list and got even whiter. "Harry Shannon? No chance it was someone else?" He nodded a few times and added, "I might have something to talk with you about in a few minutes. Are you going to be at the office? Good. I'll call you if it pans out."

158

He hung up and looked at his kids.

Aimee spoke up first. "Harry Shannon?"

"They've identified the body they found last night. The third victim of the Horseman Killer. The exact same MO. It was Harry Shannon."

Shane let out a soft gasp, looking like he might throw up.

"I want both of you home by sundown," Alan said sternly. "I mean it. No crap. You understand me?" They both nodded. "And one more thing. You leave the investigation to the police. I'm glad you found this, Shane, but you stick to your English paper. Whoever is out there is dangerous, and the last thing I ever want to do is answer a call from Ed Burroughs telling me he thinks he's identified one of your bodies."

His voice broke on the last word.

They headed for home, the sky darkening substantially. Clouds were roiling across the heavens and threatening a serious blow. The wind was kind enough to push Shane and Aimee from behind, practically forcing them to go faster.

Just as they were finally reaching their block, Aimee let out a moan. "I'm such a dumbass. . . ."

Shane was tempted to agree at least half the time but wasn't sure what today's reason was. "What?"

"I was supposed to meet up with Stasia and I forgot." She nodded to the front of their house, where

Stasia was standing, arms crossed over her chest, eyes glittering.

Shane found it moderately annoying that Stasia could look that good in a bad mood. He was beginning to think she'd look good soaking in a puddle of mud. The worst part was that it wasn't just that she was beautiful. She was smart, and funny, and sometimes seemed even more like him than, well, *him.*

Aimee ran ahead to talk to Stasia, and by the time Shane caught up, his sister was already giving the fast version of what they'd gone through. Shane nodded a few times when Stasia looked his way but otherwise let his sister talk. After what the tree had said to Aimee, he didn't want to give his sister even the tiniest reason to think it might be true. They went inside while Aimee told the rest, leading up to the bit about Harry Shannon. Grief washed over Stasia's face when she heard the news.

"God, he was kind of a nut, but he was a cool old guy," she said. Then she turned to Shane. "Where's this list?"

"He gave it to our dad."

Shane frowned. "Please. You think I would give him the only one? I copied it over before I left the town hall. I figured we were going to tell him and if I gave him the list, he'd keep it."

"Can I see it?" Stasia asked.

He slid the copy out of his back pocket and handed it to her. Stasia unfolded the paper and started scanning names. At first she just gave a quick glance, but then she looked again and swore quietly.

"Stasia? What's wrong?" He moved beside her to look at the list.

Stasia shook her head, eyes wider than usual, and took a few deep breaths, trying to calm herself. "Hasselbeck."

"I'm sorry?"

"Hasselbeck, Hasselbeck! Theodore Hasselbeck!" Her voice cracked and rose by a full octave, and Shane looked at her, wondering exactly when she'd lost the ability to speak in regular terms.

"What about him?" That was Aimee, who was as puzzled as he was.

Stasia looked from Aimee back to Shane, her eyes blinking fast and her skin the color of porcelain. "My grandmother . . . my father's mother . . . was Dorothea Hasselbeck. Both sides of his family have been in the hollow forever." She shook her head. "Shit. Hasselbeck."

Aimee's mouth dropped open. "Oh, Stasia. Damn . . ."

Shane stared at the list in her hands and at the name that had upset her so much. *Theodore Hasselbeck.*

"My father," Stasia whispered. "The Horseman will be hunting my dad."

Cold dread unlike anything Shane had ever known crept up the back of his neck. He took the list from Stasia and stood close to her, so close that any other day he would have been struck mute by being so near. Her eyes met his and Shane spoke the words he knew they were all thinking.

"Not just your father. He'll be hunting you."

Aimee stunned Shane with how calm she stayed. Stasia got up and started pacing, but Aimee went and got the phone. "Call your father, Stasia."

Stasia nodded a quick thanks and started dialing frantically. She was so nervous, she had to start three times before she finally got it right. "He should still be at home. He isn't supposed to work until tonight."

She listened for an answer and then hung up and tried again, her face getting more panicky by slow degrees. Finally she set the phone down, her hands shaking. "I have to get home. I have to see if he's okay."

In that moment all of her sophistication was gone and she was just a little girl afraid for her father. Shane ached to grab her, hold her, make everything okay.

There was one thing he could do at least. "Let's go," he said. He lifted his book bag and slung it over his shoulder. "Safety in numbers. It's not that far and we can still deal with this before our father gets home. We really should call him, actually, but . . ."

"We can't," Aimee said, her voice firm. "He's not going to understand."

Shane knew she was right.

All the way to the Traeger house Aimee and Shane did their best to remind Stasia that their father was already telling the police about the connection. Burroughs was sure to have protection set up for her and her dad in no time.

"I don't know if the police can stop him, Shane," Stasia protested. She gave an odd, unsettling little laugh. "Hell, we know he's real, and even we don't know what he really is. But I know I don't want to take any chances."

Inside the Traeger house, Stasia called for her father but got no answer. She ran up the stairs and down to the kitchen while they waited in the living room. Shane glanced out the window, his chest tight. The clouds outside had almost made night of the day. He could barely make out the individual trees rustling in the strong winds of the backyard.

Moments later Stasia came back down, chewing her lip, then suddenly brightened when she saw a note lying on the coffee table. She grabbed it and read quickly, her eyes moving fast and her lips softly mirroring the words she read on the paper.

"He's at work. Like, four people called out at the restaurant, so it's almost down to just him and Mom." She shook her head. "I thought we had a curfew in this town. Shouldn't that apply to adults too?"

"The rules never apply the same way to adults," Aimee said, reverting for a moment to her usual rebellious self.

Shane was about to say something, but suddenly his skin prickled with cold as the temperature in the room dropped twenty, maybe thirty degrees. He glanced up sharply.

Not five feet away from Stasia stood the spectral figure of a man in colonial clothes, his entire body transparent enough that Shane could see right through him. The ghost had a narrow face, pinched with worry. His eyes were pleading, looking directly at Stasia, and his mouth was moving, but no words were coming out. No voice.

Outside, the clouds were thick and dark, but light was starting to break through.

Stasia shook her head, staring at the ghost, all her fear evaporating into a smile of wonder. Shane understood immediately, viscerally. All her life she had believed in these things that couldn't be proven, and now at last this specter had manifested right there in front of her. Even Shane felt a ripple of excitement. This was no monster, like the horrors of the supernatural they'd seen in the past few days. It was a spirit, the shade of a man long dead. A window into life after death.

"I can't understand you. I can't hear you," Stasia told the apparition.

The ghost closed its eyes and shook its head. It spoke again, looking at Stasia with near desperation in its eyes. Shane studied the face, which seemed oddly familiar. It only took him a moment to figure it out.

"Wait!" Shane moved toward the ghost, his pulse racing as he finally placed the mouth, the eyes, and the nose, that familiar facial structure. It reminded him so much of Stasia's father. "Are you . . . ? Are you Theodore Hasselbeck?"

The ghost nodded quickly, smiling with relief. It started trying to speak again. Then the sun broke through the clouds. And the ghost was gone.

CHAPTER
TWELVE

AIMEE RESISTED THE urge to sigh into the phone. "Dad, I promise you we're being careful. We haven't left Stasia's house." That was a lie. Shane was on his way to the library to take a look at the journals of Washington Irving. She realized that telling her father a lie at this point might get her in deeper trouble and corrected herself. "Wait, no, I meant to say I haven't left. Shane took a quick run over to the library before it closes. He wants to look at those journals Eunice mentioned.

"Dad. Dad. No, Dad, he had to go over there. He needed to look up stuff for his report. The curfew doesn't stop us from having to go to school, unfortunately. No, I know that's not funny. Anyway, it's still daytime. Shane said he'd call you for a ride when he's done.

"Did you talk to Chief Burroughs? Did you tell him about Stasia's family? Is he going to do anything about it?" Finally she nodded and smiled. "I'll tell her, Dad. I love you. I'll be home. I'll call you when I get there, okay? Okay. Bye." Aimee set down the phone. "Stasia! Where are you?"

Stasia called down from her bedroom and Aimee walked upstairs, wondering if she were walking through the ghost as she went. Would she know? Would it hurt the ghost of Theodore Hasselbeck if she did? She had no idea and didn't want to dwell on the notion either way.

Aimee found Stasia on her bed with a dozen old books scattered around her. Weird—it was such a Shane moment. Her best friend, wild girl of Sleepy Hollow High, was also a closet nerd.

"So I talked to my dad again and he talked to the police chief and there's going to be a squad car coming over here. One is going over to the restaurant too," Aimee explained. "But my dad thinks you should call your dad. Burroughs is taking what Shane found out seriously, but he's also ready to shoot someone from the way my dad's talking. The big boys of the press are like, everywhere."

Stasia nodded, grabbing the phone from next to her bed. "Did the police talk to my dad yet?"

"I don't think so; that's why you're supposed to call him, in case it takes them too long. Let him know they're enforcing the curfew for everyone now. Not just for teenagers." Aimee couldn't help a brief flash of a smile at that. "Tell him they're probably going to make him close up for the night."

Stasia seemed calmer than before, but just barely. Aimee waited while Stasia talked to her father, cringing at the barely restrained fear in her friend's voice. Stasia was trying hard not to panic, but it wasn't easy. They both knew that if the Horseman came for Stasia or her father, a couple of police officers weren't likely to stop him. Somehow Aimee didn't think the Horseman would even notice if the police put a couple of bullets into him.

Stasia talked breathlessly, letting her father know what was going on and making him promise to come home soon and be as safe as possible, to watch his butt and wait for the police to give him an escort. When she hung up, she seemed a lot more like herself. She was the one who looked at Aimee and started the conversation they'd begun when Shane decided to go to the library.

"So, we were talking about the way the Horseman's been playing with you and Shane."

"Yeah," Aimee agreed. "I don't get it. My mother used to say she had family from around here, way back. Believe me, I've already considered the possibility that Shane and I are on the Horseman's hit list too."

Stasia waved the suggestion away. "If you were descended from one of the town council, he'd probably just have killed you when he had the chance, right?"

Aimee shuddered. "Yeah. Don't sound so upbeat about it."

"I'm upbeat about him *not* killing you, Aimes." Stasia threw a pillow at her. "I was thinking, though. I mean, do you remember when you first moved in? When we were first hanging out, you told me about the night you got to the hollow. All those lights blew out, all that weird stuff . . . I mean, it happened literally when you rolled into town."

Aimee felt cold. "What are you saying?"

Stasia shrugged one shoulder. "Well, all of this stuff did kind of coincide with you guys moving here. And the Horseman's paying you an awful lot of attention. You're not going to like hearing it, but now that you've got me thinking about it, I'm wondering if you're not even more connected to this than we've even considered. I mean, what if you guys moving to the hollow was actually what started it all? The trigger?"

"But . . . why us?" Aimee asked, her voice a tiny rasp.

Stasia could only turn up her hands. "I don't know. But I think we need to find out."

Shane's head throbbed from eyestrain and lack of sleep, but he felt alert and ready to read everything in the entire library if he had to. It hadn't been hard to get in to see the Irving papers. He'd taken a cue from his sister and lied through his teeth, claiming he was doing research for his paper for school.

He was sitting at a large table in a claustrophobic room. He would have preferred the main library, but the documents he was looking through were beyond rare, one-of-a-kind items. The librarians might have been a little slack in leaving them unattended with him, but they weren't stupid.

He reached for the next one and got lucky, opening

the book to what seemed like a solid place to start. Washington Irving wrote in his journals in a tight, precise scribble. The notes were apparently research into the entire area's vast history of unusual events.

He recognized almost word for word one of the early paragraphs from the story that had inspired his research. It read: *Some say that the place was bewitched by a high German doctor during the early days of the settlement; others, that an old Indian chief, the prophet or wizard of his tribe, held his powwows there before the country was discovered by Master Hendrick Hudson. Certain it is, the place still continues under the sway of some witching power that holds a spell over the minds of the good people, causing them to walk in a continual reverie. They are given to all kinds of marvelous beliefs; are subject to trances and visions; and frequently see strange sights, and hear music and voices in the air. The whole neighborhood abounds with local tales, haunted spots, and twilight superstitions; stars shoot and meteors glare oftener across the valley than in any other part of the country, and the nightmare, with her whole nine fold, seems to make it the favorite scene of her gambols.*

The very next page had a description of the Headless Horseman himself: *The dominant spirit, however, that haunts this enchanted region, and seems to be commander in chief of all the powers of the air, is the apparition of a figure on horseback without a head. It is said by some to be the ghost of a Hessian trooper, whose head had been carried away by a cannonball, in some nameless battle during the Revolutionary War, and who is ever and anon seen by the country folk, hurrying along in the gloom of night, as if on the wings of the wind. His haunts are not confined to the valley, but extend at times to the adjacent roads, and especially to the vicinity of a church at no great distance. Indeed, certain of the most authentic historians of those parts, who have been careful in collecting and collating the floating facts concerning this specter, allege that the body of the trooper having been buried in the church yard, the ghost rides forth to the scene of battle in nightly quest of his head, and that the rushing speed with which he sometimes passes along the hollow, like a midnight blast, is owing to his being belated, and in a hurry to get back to the churchyard before daybreak.*

Finding a churchyard from the revolutionary era could be a mess, but there might be one around. He figured he'd have to look over the local tourist maps of the area, see if he could find that churchyard and maybe a hint about how to stop the creature. On the other hand, there was no proof that what Irving had written was complete truth. He might just have taken what he wanted of the legends and made the rest of it up. Shane saw where two lines of the script had been marked out roughly at the spot where he spoke of the Horseman's legend. He doubted the bit about the cannonball having taken off the Horseman's head. The decapitation seemed too clean for that.

Just remembering the bloodless stump where the

Horseman's head should have been made his heart stutter in his chest.

Washington Irving apparently didn't mind correcting himself or rambling on paper. There were notes and scribbles in every margin, some of them looking like they'd been added later and some obviously written at the same time, in the same precise script.

"Goblins, perhaps? And, *"With a few changes, the tree could make for lovely atmosphere."* He wondered if the author was referring to the whispering tree and remembered that in Irving's story, the Headless Horseman was often seen hanging around a tree called Major André's tree, where apparently a British officer had been put to death during the Revolutionary War. He pushed the notion aside, not wanting to get completely distracted by the tree when the Headless Horseman was the prime issue. The deadly one.

After scanning a few more pages Shane gave up on the book and reached for a sheaf of papers held together with twine. The pages spilled out as he lifted them and he saw, to his pleasant surprise, a long-hand version of the story, or rather more parts of it, with sizable portions scratched out.

On those pages there were more hand-scrawled notes, some so cryptic they meant nothing. He ran across a word he'd never seen before and which, apparently, Washington Irving was also unfamiliar with. The author had written it down half a dozen times on the pages. Often with additional notes. One in particular caught his eye: *ACEPHELOS? AKEPHELOS? What is this creature I keep hearing mentioned in hushed whispers? Something to do with that roustabout Crane, from what I gather, but no one is willing to say exactly what. I'm wondering about it too much. Perhaps if I ply Mickle with a few pints of ale. The man cannot hold his ale well at all.*

And there it was. A little taste of the proof behind Shane's theory. Ichabod Crane was mentioned as well as the librarian's ancestor. With a grim smile Shane made quick notes in his notebook.

More papers and more research and slowly he began to discover further clues. Names were mentioned and a connection made, if he was reading between the lines properly. It looked like all of the town council had been involved to one extent or another with Ichabod Crane. . . .

When his cell phone rang, he let out a yelp. The silence in the small office of the library had been almost complete. "Hello?"

"Shane? Are you still at the library? It's starting to get late."

"Dad, there's still a couple of hours of daylight left."

"You might want to look outside. There's maybe an hour before dark. Stay where you are until I can pick you up. The state police are involved now, and Burroughs isn't kidding around anymore if he called in the state boys. Local police don't ever like to have to ask for help from another law enforcement agency, believe me. I'm going to pick you up, then swing by Stasia's and get Aimee—"

"I thought she was staying over there."

"So did she."

His father's tone left no room for discussion. Shane said his goodbyes and looked at the pages on the table. Somehow he must have knocked them around when he was answering the phone because a new page was in front of him.

There are more ghosts, imps, and demons in this region's local lore than in a dozen other towns this size. Shane sat up and paid closer attention to the writer's words. *It seems there's a story for nearly every household in the area, and not a few of them mention the same goblin as the others. The only unifying character from the local legends is that of the headless Hessian. He seems to simply be larger in the minds of the local folk than any of the others. The spectre was seen almost everywhere, but oddly, he also seems to have vanished nearly at the same time as I. Crane, the schoolteacher. I cannot help but wonder if the people of Sleepy Hollow fell victim to some odd jest on the part of the man. Most agree he was not a typical schoolmaster. Still, he should add flavor to the story, and I think I shall use him as the hero of my tale. If the Horseman did not do away with him in reality, he shall nevertheless do so in my story.*

There was more, but Shane didn't have the chance to read it. The librarian opened the door and smiled apologetically.

"I know you're trying to help your father out, but we're closing."

"Oh. Okay. Thanks."

The woman waited while he gathered his belongings. He thanked her again and left the library, waiting outside for his ride. The sun was a lot lower than he'd expected, long shadows reaching across the street. The town seemed eerily deserted, as though everyone had left while he was inside. Nearly all of the cars that passed by him were state or local police cruisers, and the rest were TV crews in cars and vans with camera cranes mounted on top.

Sleepy Hollow was no longer as peaceful as its name suggested. Shane wondered if it ever would be again.

Aimee looked at the books spread across Stasia's bed and desk and shook her head in surrender. "Look, let's focus on the ghost. We know who he is, and it's obvious he's trying to tell you something. He wouldn't be trying so hard if there wasn't some way to get his point across."

Stasia nodded her agreement. "Yeah, but it's no help if I can't just, y'know, summon him up out of thin air. If he really is the ghost of my ancestor, then he must have been haunting this place forever. There were always stories of the place being haunted, but as far as I know, no one ever actually *saw* him before. So why now? And if he's working so hard to communicate with me, why'd he disappear like that?"

Aimee thought back to their run-in with the ghost.

175

"I thought it was because the sun came out," she said. "I mean, that's right when he went away."

Stasia frowned.

"It was cloudy," Aimee reminded her. "And then the sun came out and he disappeared. Aren't ghosts usually seen at night? Maybe he was trying to talk to you and you could see him because it was so cloudy. Then the sky cleared and the sun came through the windows and . . . he was gone." Aimee shrugged. "This is your thing, not mine."

Stasia nodded. "Maybe, but I definitely think you're right."

"So if we make the room dark enough . . ." Aimee didn't see where that would be a problem. The sun was setting outside, and the woods in the back of Stasia's place had become a dark pattern against the encroaching night. "Okay, maybe the dark part will take care of itself. Where was the place that creeped you out the most with the cold spots?"

"Well, it was pretty bad in the attic last week. . . ."

"So let's try there and see what we get." Aimee went out into the hall and started toward the attic and Stasia followed.

The dusty attic sprawled the entire length and width of the house. A tall window at either end provided a glimmer of light from outside, but a bank of clouds had darkened the sky even as dusk swallowed the last of the daylight. Inside, two bare bulbs hung down from the ceiling, illuminating the boxes of faded memories and the furniture long since abandoned by the Traeger family and the Hasselbecks before them.

Once they were up the stairs, Stasia pulled the chains to turn off the two lights. Almost instantly the air in the attic grew cold. Aimee shivered and hugged herself. She held her breath and watched as a kind of silver mist pooled in the center of the attic and the ghost of Theodore Hasselbeck manifested in the space between the two girls.

It gazed at Stasia, its long thin fingers held out toward her.

CHAPTER THIRTEEN

THE GHOST'S LIPS moved, forming words that remained silent. Aimee and Stasia both moved closer, but the only sounds were their own breathing and the creak of the old house in the wind. The spirit of Theodore Hasselbeck seemed as frustrated as Aimee herself felt.

Night had fallen just in the last few moments, but now the cloud bank outside the windows cleared and the moon broke through, its golden light limning the entire attic in a shimmering glow. Moonlight splashed across the floor, illuminating the girls and passing right through the ghost.

The moment it did, they could hear his voice.

" . . . *in danger, child. You must flee this place, this wretched town.*" The words were faint, soft as the wind outside the house, but they were words.

Stasia stared at him, eyes wide with emotion. Aimee felt it too, the kindness of this ancient specter.

"I can't," Stasia said. "My father would never go

without an explanation. And I won't leave him here. We have to stop the Horseman."

The ephemeral mist that constituted the phantom's form shuddered, churning like a rolling fog. The fear was visible in his face. *"That one, he's a demon. You dare not face him."*

Aimee moved beside Stasia and stared at the ghost. The dark pits of its eyes made that spectral face look almost skeletal. "We have to. But we need help. Can you tell us anything?"

The clouds covered the moon momentarily, and like a radio picking up bad reception, the words Hasselbeck spoke were lost in silence though his lips still moved. When the moon broke through again, the words drifted back as they had faded, so faint it was a strain to hear them at all. *". . . I could not come here before; I was lost and I did not need to, but I sensed when the vow was broken, when Acephelos rose again and released the demons."*

Aimee tried to speak, to make a coherent sentence, but Stasia made a gesture for her to shut up.

"What vow was broken?"

"We made the vow. All of us. DeMarchant, Shannon, Winthorpe . . . all of us. We struck a deal with the Horseman, you see. And all because of that devil, Ichabod Crane."

"What?" Aimee asked. "Please, we don't understand."

The ghost turned those pitted black eyes upon her and its baleful gaze froze the breath in her lungs. *"Crane came from a fine family, but his birth was their darkest hour. He performed dark magicks to bring him whatever he wished. Love. Riches. And when he offered to improve the town's fortunes in the same manner, we dared not ask how he would do it. He was as good as his word. A rarity for Mr. Crane. It was only later that we understood that he had made the town wealthy to corrupt our hearts, so our own greed would blind us to the darker works he wrought in that little stone house."*

Aimee's face must have looked blank. The ghost of Theodore Hasselbeck sneered at her in disgust.

"You don't understand. But you will."

In the moonlight the specter reached out his translucent hands and *touched* them. There was no contact, only cold. And then . . . images rushed into Aimee's mind, and she was lost to the world.

Ichabod Crane stoked the fire in his chimney, the flames lifting high enough to make even the darkest corners of the room seem as if they stood in the noonday sun. The air was oppressively hot, leaving Crane and his guest, Baltus Van Tassel, sweating heavily. Crane gazed into the fire for a long moment, as though fascinated by the black streaks of soot on the stone within. He stood then and plucked at the knees of his trousers, smoothing them.

"What is this all about?" Van Tassel demanded. Sweat dripped down the side of his face and slid into his high collar. The buckles of his shoes gleamed in the firelight, but otherwise he was clad in rigid black and white. His beard quivered as he spoke. "Why did you call me here so late on this miserably cold night?"

Ichabod removed his spectacles and slid them into his pocket. He looked at the man and smiled thinly. "Why else? Because you need my help."

A draft blew through the small house, rattling the windows and setting the lantern to swaying upon its hook by the door. It cast a wavering shadow upon an old rocking chair in the corner.

Van Tassel shifted uncomfortably. "What could you possibly help me with?"

"What you and every other member of the town council has asked me to help you with, each thinking to save his own miserable hide and damn the consequences for the township."

Crane stretched and moved away from the fireplace. The old floorboards creaked, dust sifting down in the narrow spaces between them. At a sideboard he uncorked a jug and poured himself a glass of sweet wine. He offered another to Van Tassel, who declined. The thin man slid a watch out of the pocket of his vest, tapped the crystal on its face, and adjusted its fob.

Van Tassel reached up to smooth his beard, waiting impatiently. He gazed at his walking stick, which stood by the door, as though longing to leave that place.

"Each of you has asked that I help drive the demons from Sleepy Hollow. Well, I have found a way to do it." Crane raised his eyebrows.

"Surely you can't be serious."

"Of course I'm serious, Baltus. I've told all the others and they've agreed that the best way to remove the problem in Sleepy Hollow is to engage a . . . specialist. I have discovered just such an agent and am prepared to employ him."

"Ichabod, how do you propose to hire someone at your wages? You're a schoolmaster, not a landowner." Baltus's voice had taken on a gentle chiding tone. "Unless all the tales of your family's hidden wealth are true?"

Crane waved his long, thin fingers in the air. "Oh, I'm far from a wealthy man, my friend. But I shall pay, Baltus. I shall pay with the wages of what I've sown."

"What does that mean?" Van Tassel asked, flushing in alarm.

"You know precisely what I mean. The prosperity of this town and of the council in particular has been brought about by my hands and no other. Your crops were failing, your livestock malnourished and worth little save as leather before I came here."

"Surely you can't believe that you are responsible for all of our good fortunes?" Baltus laughed, a deep, robust sound that fit his portly frame. The fob from his own watch jangled quietly. As he turned from the fire, its light threw half of his face in shadows.

Crane narrowed his gaze and glared at the man. "Must we play games, Baltus? Must you constantly pretend ignorance? Do you think lies will save your soul?"

"I refuse to sit here and listen to flings against my character, Crane!" he sputtered, the pointed ends of his mustache curling upward with his sneer.

"Baltus, when I was a young man, growing up in this town, there was nothing worth owning. Had I not worked a few simple spells to bring the right sort of help, you would be the mayor of little more than a collection of mud huts." Crane's angular face stretched into a decidedly unpleasant grin. "It was I who performed the rituals, who prepared offerings to the creatures of the pit, who called forth the naiads and dryads and summoned the spirits of the harvest to bring about bountiful crops in this pathetic little valley. My power brought forth the aid needed to make Sleepy Hollow a place where the worst concern was whether to milk the cows once a day or twice. Without me all of you would be starving by now."

Van Tassel trembled with the vehemence of his denial. He gripped the carved arms of the chair in which he sat. There was a copper pot near the fire, and in it his reflection was almost monstrous. "That's preposterous! Such talk is blasphemy."

Crane laughed, rolling up the stiff cuffs of his shirt-sleeves. "Oh, it's blasphemy now, is it? Once upon a time you called such works miracles and were properly thankful for them. You forget yourself, Baltus. You forget in whose home you now sit. Perhaps you are merely practicing your denials for others' ears, but do not inflict them upon me a moment longer.

"You knew, Baltus, all of you knew. I performed rituals on your own farm, danced in the light of the full moon and invoked names not meant to be spoken by mere mortals. You saw me, Van Tassel, and your wife saw me as well. Even your plow horses saw me!" Crane smirked, leaned in closer to where Baltus Van Tassel sat, and placed a hand on each of the armrests of the wooden chair. "You knew, and you wife knew, and lovely Katrina knew."

"You're mad, Crane."

"No, Your Honor, I am wise and powerful. You wouldn't be the first to confuse the two."

Van Tassel nodded slowly. "Fine, then, Crane. But if you claim the credit, you must also bear the blame. Or would you deny that you must also then be held responsible for the recent deaths in Sleepy Hollow? If we're to thank you for our good fortunes, we shall curse you as a witch and punish you for our misfortunes as well. If you have brought us blessings, certainly you have also summoned the monsters that haunt us all?"

"*All*, Mayor Van Tassel? Surely not. Have you noticed that the council is safe? That your family has been spared attack by the spirits that roam the region?"

"Mere coincidence . . ." He spoke the words, but his voice was unsure.

"Hardly, Baltus. These creatures demanded a certain . . . freedom they have not had before, and they have brought others of their ilk besides." He waved his hands dismissively again. "A small oversight on my part, I assure you, but one that I can rectify. No, Baltus, you and yours and the families of all the council are safe because I made sure of it. Kill me and that assurance is gone; lock me in the stockade and I will let them loose to wreak their vile ways wherever they see fit instead of giving them choice victims only."

"You . . ." Van Tassel sputtered. "You chose who the monsters attacked?"

"On occasion. There was a certain blacksmith who offended me." Crane leaned back. His smile grew sly and secretive. "You'll notice that it's only Brom Van Brunt at the forge these days. What a pity his father simply disappeared. . . ."

"Merciful God, Crane! The council would see you in irons either way if they knew."

"Ah, but they don't know, Baltus, and a wise man knows when to keep his tongue if he would safeguard his life and that of his lovely wife." He grinned again. "And the comely daughter of that very wise man need not be filled with worry, for she will soon be betrothed to me."

Baltus stared at Ichabod Crane with eyes glinting with rage. "Is that your price for the salvation of Sleepy Hollow? Your payment for rescuing us from the evils you yourself brought upon our heads?"

"Not at all, Baltus. I will require more than a mere dowry to save this village from its fate. I must make sacrifices of my own to summon the one who can put an end to the horrible misfortunes befalling this place."

"You would summon another demon to put down

the very demons you've brought to this village?"

"Not just any demon, Van Tassel. A very special being, one who can be called forth only with great risk. But I am more than capable of handling the challenge."

"What would you call forth, Lucifer himself?"

"Nothing so drastic, but close enough for our needs. Once I have made my bargain with him, he shall protect Sleepy Hollow from any more mischief by the lesser imps and sprites."

"And how will you bind him to do your bidding?" Baltus asked. "Does this monster of yours need gold or a portion of the harvests?"

"No, old friend, the ritual to call forth Acephelos requires a sacrifice far greater. He requires a human life."

Baltus Van Tassel rose from his seat, nodding as if in contemplation even as he sidled closer to the door of the madman's home. "Surely you don't mean to kill a citizen of Sleepy Hollow? Perhaps one of those savage Iroquois?"

"Hmm. The thought of the savages never occurred to me." Crane paused. His hand rested in the shadows thrown by the raging fire, a dark pit of shadow that Baltus had seen earlier but given no thought to. "Perhaps that would work. . . ."

Baltus exhaled. "You would have us capture one of them, then? I suspect we can have one rounded up in a day or so."

Crane nodded, no longer smiling. "Yes, that might be for the best." He walked away from his darkened little corner, and Baltus Van Tassel saw that he held one hand close by his side, out of sight. "There's only one problem with that notion, Baltus."

The schoolteacher drew a long, wicked blade from the shadows.

"What? No, Ichabod! Have you gone mad?"

Crane laughed softly. "Not at all, Baltus, calm yourself. This is merely to show you. The sacrifice must be beyond precious. As I am the one who makes the summoning, I am the one who must sacrifice the most."

"Dear Lord, Ichabod." Baltus Van Tassel's voice shook with the release of stress. "You mean to give your own life?"

Ichabod Crane frowned. "The ritual demands that the summoner make himself a sacrifice. That is the price of bringing in the demon that will drive off all the other supernatural beasts, all the monsters that I summoned in my folly."

"Ichabod . . . I had no idea." Baltus's whole expression changed, relief washing over his features and a glint of admiration coming into his eyes. "I've no idea what to say to you, my friend. That you would sacrifice so much for us all. But . . . what of your words only moments ago? If the price of this is your life, how can you marry—?"

And then Ichabod Crane lunged forward.

Baltus gasped and staggered backward, trying to ward off the attack. Crane slid the blade past his shaking hand with the ease of a skilled swordsman. The dagger's edge sliced through Van Tassel's neck with ease, cutting veins and arteries and severing his throat, leaving a gasping wail of breath and twin gouts of hot blood in its wake.

Van Tassel fell to his knees, trying futilely to stop the crimson wash that ran down his chest, eyes bulging. The draft whistled through cracks in the windows. The whole cottage shook. The lantern creaked upon its hook and the shadows danced.

"Baltus, old friend, why would I give my own life when I can substitute yours?" Crane asked, smiling. "My hold on the darkness is strong enough that I can afford to alter the ritual. Such is the power in my hands. And really, when have you ever known me to follow the rules?"

Van Tassel's hands fell away as he weakened, and Crane took advantage of the moment, whipping the ritual blade through the air and hacking at bone, muscle, and gristle. Van Tassel's head fell to the ground, and a moment later his body followed suit.

"Rules are for the weak."

Images shifted, the world flashed by, night became day became night and again and again as Aimee and Stasia stood mesmerized in the attic. Soon enough the visions they saw stabilized, and the knowledge the ghost of Stasia's ancestor sent to them continued on, filling their heads.

The Headless Horseman was worse than all of the other horrors Crane's occult dabblings had attracted to

Sleepy Hollow. The people of the village were in a panic. The headless demon rode the night, charging across fields and storming through the township itself, its fury unrelenting. Mayor Van Tassel was missing, and his great black mastiff, the brute affectionately called Hizzoner, had gone mad, howling insanely into the night and roaming the woods in search of his master. It quickly came to pass that people dreaded the sound of the animal's beastly cries, for wherever they were heard, the horseman inevitably struck. Half the men of the town council were dead, victims of the marauding Horseman, who sought, it seemed, to find his head and would take others until he found his own.

For nearly a fortnight the insanity continued, and finally the council went to Ichabod Crane, begging his help. Though they would deny it to family and friends, even to their wives, they all knew the truth of what had brought them both fortune and ill fate. Now they had no choice but to go to the man who was their savior and their tormentor alike. Arrangements were made. Crane managed to settle a meeting place in the heart of the woods, a neutral place where the council and the Horseman could parley and the demon would not harm them. A circle would be placed in the ground, a ward to protect them as they bargained with the creature.

Crane's help came at a price, of course. He demanded the value of Van Tassel's land in gold. Each member of the council had to forfeit a sizable portion of his own monies to gather the payment. Yet the cost would have been far higher if the blacksmith had not suggested a ruse. The council forged coins of lead and dipped them in gold to deceive Ichabod Crane.

Now they waited in the woods, the surviving members of the council, hoping that Crane would not realize their duplicity until it was too late. Night had fallen and the moon was full, and Ichabod Crane was nowhere to be seen. But as Theodore Hasselbeck began to complain of his absence, a rider approached.

They knew right away that the rider was not Crane. The horse was no less than twenty-two hands high and muscled as few animals in the region were muscled in these days of peace. The rider approached at a slow pace and stopped just outside the clearing where the council waited. That much, at least, Ichabod Crane had done properly. The circle was there and the monstrous thing that approached came no closer than its edge.

Harold Shannon backed away from the rider, his voice breaking as he cried out. "He's got no head! He *is* a demon!"

Hasselbeck clutched the man's shoulder and pulled him back as he tried to run. "Be still, you fool! Should you break the circle of protection, he'll have your head as his own!"

In the end it was Hasselbeck who was forced to speak as their leader, though he hardly felt up to it. There was something deeply horrifying about the creature itself that made even the defiled state of its flesh pale in comparison.

The Horseman rode around their circle of protection, his gigantic stallion stomping the ground impatiently. Hasselbeck and the others consulted in whispered tones as the beast and its rider paced around them, satisfied for the moment at least to wait them out.

"Why do you torment our village? What have we done to draw your wrath?" Hasselbeck called to the demon. "Crane performed his ritual to draw you here so you would drive off the other evils that plague us, yet you have only joined them. Is there some price unpaid, some bargain that might be struck to keep you and all the other horrors away from Sleepy Hollow? Whatever the cost, we shall pay it."

The Horseman paused and seemed to regard him, though without a head it was difficult to know for certain. Hasselbeck felt a surge of nausea as he stared at the bloody stump of his neck. But the Horseman made no attempt to communicate.

"Damn that Ichabod Crane! Where is he now, when we need him?"

At the sound of the schoolteacher's name the Horseman stood taller in his saddle, his body turned toward Hasselbeck and the space where his head should have been facing the man. Theodore had never been more terrified in his entire life.

The horseman reached down to an antiquated

saddlebag near his left leg and drew forth a severed head. They all recognized the face of Goodman Wilson, who had been missing for over a week. The Horseman threw his grisly prize and it tumbled inside the circle. The councilmen, Hasselbeck included, let out cries of panic and hastily backed away.

Theodore forced himself to concentrate. "We don't understand. You want a . . . wait. You want your head back?"

The Horseman tugged on the reins and his black horse neighed and reared up onto its hind legs. Hasselbeck nodded. That must be it.

"We would gladly give it, but we neither have your . . . your head, nor would we know where to begin looking. The only man who would know where to find it is Ichabod Crane, and he is missing!"

The Headless Horseman drew his saber with frightening speed and pointed it at each of the men. They quailed, but none were foolish enough to run. The circle of protection that Ichabod Crane had placed on the forest clearing was all that kept them safe.

"Isn't there any other way to appease you?"

The Horseman trotted the horse to the nearest tree and swung the saber in half a dozen swift, efficient strokes, hacking at the bark. By the light of the moon they could all see very clearly what the demon had carved into the wood. Two letters. *I. C.*

"You want Ichabod Crane?" Hasselbeck swallowed hard, his heart hammering to escape from his chest.

The Horseman only sat astride his mount and seemed to regard them. Then he reached beneath his cloak and produced yet another head, this one seemingly from the shadows of his own substance. The demon tossed the second head upon the ground and Hasselbeck stepped back, startled. This one belonged to the minister who had come to town and believed he could drive the monsters away.

"We do not know where Crane is! He's fled Sleepy Hollow. He has run from here and we've heard no news of him, though we have looked. You may rest assured we have looked, sir!"

The horseman's mount pranced impatiently and through the greatest of efforts, Theodore stayed his place.

It was Adam DeMarchant who moved up beside Hasselbeck to whisper in his ear. "A solemn vow, Theo. We shall make him a promise that Crane shall never be allowed to return to Sleepy Hollow, that he will never have a home here as long as the Horseman stays away."

Hasselbeck nodded. DeMarchant was on to something, but there was more to it. It was desperate, but he would try anything.

"We can promise you this," he called to the headless creature. "A solemn vow to which we all shall swear. Should Ichabod Crane ever return to Sleepy Hollow— if any of his bloodline dares to set foot within our township—we shall deliver them to you."

The Horseman paused a moment, holding his horse steady, and then bowed low in agreement.

"And the bargain you made with Crane? Will you still honor it?" Theodore Hasselbeck held his breath as soon as he had spoken. Fear made him stink with sweat in the chilled night air.

The Horseman moved forward, his saber slicing the air, and Theodore stood his ground not from bravery, but from the paralysis of terror. The saber drove into the skull of the beheaded preacher and then the Horseman dropped it into his bag. He moved forward again, brushing past Hasselbeck with scarcely a hair's breadth between the stallion and his own flesh. Whatever the circle was supposed to do, it failed. Hasselbeck listened to the rest of the council as they screamed in fear and retreated.

The Horseman stopped at the head of Goodman Wilson and skewered it from his saddle. He casually placed it back into the saddlebag and slid his blade free, ignoring the screaming councilmen. He turned his mount and rode back to gaze down upon Theodore Hasselbeck.

Theodore waited, half expecting his head to be taken as a final prize, but instead the Horseman slid gracefully down from the black stallion and faced him. He bowed again and Theo's eyes were drawn to the raw, bloody stump of a neck that hid within the shadows of his mantle.

"And is there another price for this service, sir?"

The horseman touched him, his hand so fast that Theodore never even saw it coming, and the voice of that demon spoke to him in words that blasted like lightning strikes across his mind. *I shall drive from your hills and forests, from your streets and river, every beast and monster and flight of fancy that no longer belongs in this world. I shall give them refuge beyond the shroud of human understanding. But you have made your vow, Theodore Hasselbeck. Should Crane or his bloodline return to this place, the people of Sleepy Hollow shall give them up in sacrifice to me. Blood sacrifice. And if the vow is broken, then before I have my vengeance upon Crane's blood, I shall throw aside the shroud and let the beasts plague you once more. Then I shall hunt each of you or those of your own bloodline. It shall be their heads in payment for my own.*

Theodore fell to the ground, his mind numbed by the cold, sepulchral voice that rampaged through his skull. He thought that he had felt fear before in his life, but he was mistaken. Nothing he had ever experienced had come close. The touch of the creature was worse than death: it promised suffering through centuries of torment, the likes of which Hades itself would be hard pressed to match.

So close to the demon for the first time, Hasselbeck noticed the ring it wore on the third finger of its left hand. He knew that ring.

It belonged to Baltus Van Tassel.

A moment later the horseman climbed back atop his steed and rode off, not another word or gesture made.

The clouds hid the moon again for the briefest moment, but it was long enough to break the trance.

Aimee stared at the ghost, chills running through her. She glanced over at Stasia and saw that her friend seemed just as disoriented as she felt. Then at last Stasia met her gaze.

"So, the Horseman is this . . . Van Tassel guy?" Stasia asked.

Aimee nodded slowly. "I think so. Or maybe partly him and partly . . . something else. Somehow Crane made the Horseman when he killed Van Tassel. And the dog . . . Hizzoner . . . it's been searching for him ever since Ichabod Crane killed him." She spoke softly, absorbing the information.

Hasselbeck's ghost silently clapped his spectral hands. The moonlight washed through the attic again. He could speak further if he wanted to.

"But how did Ichabod Crane get away without anyone knowing?" Aimee asked him.

It was Stasia who answered. "He was a sorcerer, and a pretty good one if he could summon so many spirits."

"Mmm. Maybe *not* so good. He couldn't control them, and more and more of the things just kept coming. And when he called up the Horseman, he blew it. You saw it just like I did. He was supposed to give his

196

own life in that ritual, let himself become the Horseman, but he substituted Van Tassel. He blew the whole deal. The moron."

"Precisely," the ghost whispered.

"So, what's the story?" Stasia asked her ancestor's spirit. "Can we get rid of the Horseman?"

Hasselbeck's ghost spoke again, the words half lost as thin clouds began to pass across the moon, but its voice was just strong enough for them to hear. *"Crane lost himself in other places. I have heard whispers of him in the afterlife. His family had long since died or departed our village. He was the last of them. But when he left Sleepy Hollow, he took another name to hide behind."* Broken clouds obscured the moon and disrupted his words, so that they could make out only some of what he said. *"Acephelos . . . summon . . . was to take his head and hide it . . ."*

Stasia nodded, listening intently, and Aimee held her breath, straining so hard to hear any words that could help them.

"Give . . . Horseman back his head and . . ."

"But it's hidden," Aimee said. "How do we find it? Do you know where it's hidden?"

"Van Tassel . . . buried without his head . . . Crane said ritual required holy ground, so it must be in a cemetery . . . a family crypt . . . Return it to him, and the covenant will be . . ."

Aimee thought the last word was *broken,* but she couldn't be sure.

The clouds thickened, completely obscuring the

moon. A storm was coming; the wind promised that. Theodore Hasselbeck continued trying to speak but failed, his words lost with the moonlight, his form fading until he could barely be seen at all. Finally he was gone.

Stasia sighed, deflating. "This isn't going to be easy. There're a lot of graveyards in Sleepy Hollow. And he said it was buried in a family crypt, but which one?"

"Well, we need the oldest ones. . . ." Aimee shrugged. "Shane has that list of old names, but it's just a beginning. If I had to bet, though, I'd want to check Crane's own family crypt first. If there is one."

"Yeah," Stasia said, her voice soft and drifting. Then she turned to Aimee, eyes intense. "We can start looking first thing in the morning. If we find it before dark, this could all be over tomorrow. But . . ."

Aimee frowned. "But what?"

"Don't you get it? Weren't you even listening?" Stasia said, biting her lip, her eyes sad. "We were talking about why the Horseman was toying with you and Shane and about how all this really started when you guys first got into town."

Ice ran down Aimee's spine. "Like we were the trigger."

Stasia nodded. "The vow the council made . . . If Crane or any of his blood ever came back to Sleepy Hollow . . ."

Aimee shook her head slowly. "It can't be. We don't have any Cranes in our family. There's got to be another reason. It . . . it can't be."

CHAPTER
FOURTEEN

"I'M SORRY I was so long getting to you, Shane." Alan's eyes were bloodshot and his clothes disheveled—the man was clearly a wreck.

"Dad, it's all right. Nothing happened. I waited right at the door of the library and there were enough police cars cruising around that no one could have gotten to me without someone noticing."

A lie, maybe, but only just barely. He'd seen the state police cars all over the center of town and probably would have been dragged away by them if he hadn't been keeping an alert eye on everything while trying to remain semi-hidden. He hadn't walked to his dad's car; he'd run. A few minutes later they'd been on their way toward Stasia's house, with his dad filling him in on the latest. Yes, the police were making threats to haul people in if they had to and they would carry out the threats in extreme cases, but mostly they were there to keep their eyes out for maniacs riding on horseback.

Burroughs intended to see the freak they were calling

the Horseman Killer taken down fast. Every major road would be monitored through the night and the side roads were all being hit as frequently as possible. Burroughs himself was taking great pleasure in making sure that the visiting journalists got themselves off the streets and settled into their hotels. He was making it a point to arrest any out of towners who were playing with his curfew. There was already one Manhattan news crew sitting behind bars. Still, catching the killer would be the best way to stop the insanity.

They moved down Broadway and turned left, heading down the side road leading to Stasia's place. At the next intersection Shane got a funny feeling in his stomach. Then he remembered what lay ahead of them. One intersection down was the spot where Hizzoner was supposed to be lurking. Shane swallowed and looked out the window, wondering if the black dog would show itself.

And saw the Headless Horseman pacing beside the car, moving alongside them from a range of around twenty yards.

"Dad! Out the window!"

His father looked where he pointed, tapping the brakes, and let out a grunt of surprise as he saw the rider on horseback only sixty feet away. "Grab the cell phone, Shane."

Shane reached for the cradle where the phone sat and unhooked the device. He watched as the horseman's steed reared up and charged toward the car.

Shane forgot all about the phone in his hands as his father gunned the engine.

"He can't seriously be trying to take on a car!" Alan Lancaster's voice was half laughing and half screaming. The horseman came closer still, the blade of his sword catching what little light was provided on the darkened road. The horse and rider cut to the right, moving alongside the station wagon on Shane's side. His father looked past him and out the passenger side window, trying to see the rider's face. "What does he look like, Shane, can you get a good look at his face?"

"Dad, he doesn't have a face! He's got no damned head!"

His father gunned the engine again, sending the car toward the crossroad ahead like a rocket. The Horseman kept pace, and Shane looked over to see they were already doing almost fifty miles an hour.

And then suddenly the horseman cut back, his stallion rearing its front hooves into the night air and the rider leaning forward on the horse's neck to compensate for the change. Shane turned to look at his father and tell him to go faster, but he never got the words out.

Hizzoner came from the darkness on his father's side of the car and slammed into the left-front quarter panel. Shane's father swerved to avoid going off the road into the trees, but it slowed them, costing precious seconds. The black dog jumped onto the hood of the moving station wagon. Its eyes burned with a deep red

201

fire and its teeth flashed, long dagger fangs that snapped and gnashed at the windshield. Thick black claws drew furrows in the paint of the old car and the monster slammed its muzzle into the glass only inches from Alan Lancaster's startled face.

The windshield spiderwebbed, lightning strikes of fracture moving out in a wave from the point where the behemoth dog's teeth scratched the glass. The dog's muzzle slammed the windshield a second time. This time the glass didn't hold.

The windshield shattered inward and Alan slammed on the brakes. Luckily Shane was wearing his seat belt. The next instant the car was off the road, tires bumping over ruts in the earth. When the car abruptly stopped, Shane felt the shoulder belt cut into skin with bruising force. Hizzoner was launched through the air, thick claws scrabbling for purchase and a snarl of fury erupting from its black lips.

Alan Lancaster's head whipped forward and cracked into the steering wheel with an audible thump. When the car came to a halt, he was unconscious. A trail of blood ran from a wound on his forehead.

Shane cursed his father's love of old cars—without air bags—and looked around for anything he could use to staunch the flow of blood. Finally he pressed his own jacket against the wound. Hizzoner reared back up from where he lay sprawled among the trees, his growl a bass so deep it could be felt as well as heard. Shane looked at the dog and then at his father. Finally his gaze fell on what seemed like his only hope. The bundle that Stasia and Aimee had made a few days earlier lay at one corner of the intersection, dangling from a low branch on a nearby tree. If the ward worked at all, it had to be better than trying to fight off the dog.

His father's forehead was still bleeding, but the flow had slowed. Shane slid out from under his father and looked outside to see Hizzoner pacing around the car. He shifted until his dad was resting as comfortably as possible and then he opened his door.

The black dog growled low and deep and moved in his direction, loping steadily, not racing. Shane waited until the animal was coming at the door from the front and braced himself. As Hizzoner moved to block the door or push through it to get to him, Shane shoved outward with all the strength he could muster and slammed the open door into the dog's head. The door buckled a bit, and he felt the impact up his arms, but Hizzoner let out a grunt and slumped back a pace or two, shaking his muzzle from side to side.

Not a ghost, Shane thought. *Some other kind of monster.*

He ran as fast as he could, feet slapping the asphalt as he tore across the intersection. Long before he reached his prize, he heard the sound of scrabbling claws digging for purchase and knew Hizzoner was after him.

Whatever was bundled into the cloth on the tree, it stank horribly. Shane grabbed the small package and pulled, snapping the branch it was attached to. He pivoted around, eyes wild, trying to find something he could use as a weapon, his fingers clutching only the small poultice and the stick it was tied to. The chances of hurting the monster with that were nonexistent. Seeing nothing, he braced himself for the impact he knew was coming.

And waited some more as the dog suddenly stopped, panting deep in its chest and tilting its head, looking for him. Shane stared, dumbfounded, as the animal looked right through him and sniffed the air, trying, it seemed, to catch his scent. He waved his hand at the animal, half expecting his fingers to be devoured. Nothing. The dog kept that same surprised expression on its face and lumbered to his left, sniffing.

Sooner or later Hizzoner was going to remember the car on the side of the road, and Shane didn't like that notion. He moved, walking sideways, toward the station wagon, his eyes never leaving the animal. He fumbled for a couple of moments before finally managing to open his door again. The dog whipped around at the sound of the car door but once again failed to see him.

Shane slid into the car and closed the door as the brute padded around the car, puzzling out where the source of the sound had been. Shane checked on his father. Alan Lancaster was still unconscious and he had a bruise growing on his forehead, but his breathing was steady and his pulse was strong.

Shane reached for the cell phone, his hands shaking. As he dialed, the animal stood nearby, panting heavily and looking for the prize it had captured and then suddenly lost.

The phone rang as Stasia and Aimee came down the stairs from the attic. Aimee still felt unsettled and dazed from their encounter with the ghost, but Stasia seemed revitalized. Aimee shook her head in amazement. *She gets off on this stuff too much. It's like she's addicted to weird.*

Stasia reached out and grabbed the phone. "Hello? Shane?" Her brow knitted and she shot Aimee a nervous glance. "Wait! Shane, slow down, what's wrong?"

"What is it?" Suddenly Aimee's own stomach was doing flip-flops.

Stasia handed her the phone, her hand trembling a bit, and then bolted up the stairs. "There's been an accident," she called out over her shoulder. "I have to gather some stuff—talk to Shane."

Shane sounded like he couldn't catch his breath, and worse, there was a savage, deep barking going on in the background that made Aimee's spine turn to ice. But somehow in a collection of broken sentences Shane managed to get out that there had been a car accident, that Hizzoner was outside the car, and that their father was unconscious.

"Stasia went to get supplies, Shane. You stay there! We'll be there as soon as we can!" She was screaming but couldn't make herself stop. Her nerves were shot

205

and she was way too terrified for her father and brother to fake calm.

"I'll wait as long as I can," her brother said, and then he hung up.

Aimee looked outside as headlights spilled into the driveway. She could see the silhouettes of Stasia's dad and possibly her mom. She swallowed hard and was about to scream for Stasia to hurry it the hell up when her friend came down the stairs with a backpack that bulged slightly and sloshed.

"Your folks just pulled up."

Stasia ran to the window and looked outside as carefully as she could. She nodded. "That's them. They're talking to the cops. Let's go."

"You don't want to tell them?"

"You think they'd let us run off to face a hellhound?"

Aimee shook her head and took a deep breath, following Stasia to the back door of the old Victorian. Stasia knew her way through the backyard even without any light, and the two of them were away from the house in a flash.

The night was miserable—the clouds had buried the moon behind a thick black caul and the wind whipped their hair across their faces. The air was unseasonably cold and neither of them had jackets, but that was the least of Aimee's concerns.

They moved as quickly as they could, which didn't feel fast enough for Aimee. The intersection finally came into view from the left, and Aimee had to force herself to breathe. It took a moment to find the station wagon in the gathering gloom. The streetlight that should have been burning at the intersection was one of the many in Sleepy Hollow that had not yet been replaced.

Stasia stopped abruptly in front of her. Aimee bumped lightly into her friend.

"There they are," Stasia whispered, just in case Hizzoner might be listening. "I don't see the dog, but I bet he's still here."

Aimee looked at the car, where it rested half in a ditch, the back wheels off the ground. She gritted her teeth, fear fading to a dull black and a dark red rage brewing up inside her. She wanted to find the black dog and kill it slowly for hurting her father. Instead she followed Stasia as she started toward the car, moving carefully and trying to look everywhere at once.

It was the longest few minutes of Aimee's life. Every move, every sound was enough to make her want to scream, but eventually they made it. Aimee opened the car door, looking quickly at her brother first. Shane looked okay but pale. She turned to her father and gasped. His skin was so white she worried that they were too late, but then she saw his eyes move beneath the lids and noticed his chest rising and falling with his breathing. Still, the wound on his forehead was angry and black with crusted blood.

Stasia assessed the situation with a calm that was

almost mercenary. "We've got all the stuff to build the wards," she said. "How's your dad?"

Shane looked from one girl to the other, almost as if he hadn't expected to see anyone. The wind caught the door and blew it farther open and Aimee glanced around, her heart thudding hard. Had she just heard something? She couldn't tell and now Shane was talking and ruining her chance to hear anything and how could he have let her father get hurt like that?

She focused on her brother's words, making up her mind to worry about tearing him apart later. "And the next thing I know, the Horseman's gone, but that damn dog is here and trying to open the car like a can of tuna. If you guys hadn't started those protection things before, we'd probably both be dead."

"Well, thank God you're both alive. I can have these up and finished in just a few minutes and then we can call for an ambulance."

"Do you need this one back?"

"No, keep it. If it's working to hide you away from that thing, then you use it and keep your dad safe. Aimee and I can handle this." Stasia dug into her backpack and cursed under her breath. "My bad, Shane. I need it back after all." She looked at Aimee and then back at Shane. "I screwed it up. I don't have all of the ingredients. I remembered the cat piss, but I left out half of the poultice."

Shane winced as Aimee reached in to grab the

208

ward. "You stay in the car with Dad, okay?" she told him. "I'll help Stasia."

Shane nodded and reached for the door, which let out a shriek of protest as he started to pull it closed.

"Be careful!" Aimee hissed. She ran toward Stasia, who took the bundle from her and moved back toward the tree Shane had plucked it from. She had crossed barely half the distance when Hizzoner came out of nowhere, charging for the car.

The beast rammed Shane's door and the entire station wagon shook from the impact. Hizzoner stalked around the front of the car, glaring at the hole he'd already punched into the fractured windshield. Without the protective ward, the black dog had the scent of its prey again.

Aimee reached into her pocket and fumbled for her spare change. "Hey! Hey, mutt!"

Hizzoner ignored her and climbed atop the hood of the station wagon, the front end groaning under his staggering weight. Aimee flung the change from her jeans as hard as she could, hoping to at least get the monster's attention. Her idea worked better than she'd ever imagined. The coins soared through the air and a quarter nailed the behemoth in the eye. Hizzoner let out a shockingly high-pitched yelp and then shifted his head to look at her.

The jet black face seemed almost featureless in the darkness except for the glowing coals of his eyes and the gleaming daggers of his teeth.

Aimee heard thunder and realized a second later

that the noise was the dog growling. "Oh, crap! Stasia, work faster!"

Hizzoner charged, and Aimee screamed, vaulting hard to the left. She felt the wind from the dog's passing, smelled the musty, decayed scent of something long dead, and watched in terror as the claws of the beast cut gashes in the pavement. The black dog roared, a sound she knew she never wanted to hear again, and scrambled around quickly for another try at her. From the corner of her eye she saw Stasia finishing the reknotting of the poultice, the remaining ingredients for the others already stuffed into her hands. Stasia didn't bother with gloves this time and the reek of stagnant cat urine wafted from her bare hands and arms.

Aimee scrambled backward across the ground, wincing at a pain in her left palm, which felt like it had been scoured by a hundred stones or so. Even in what little moonlight made it through the ominous clouds, she could see the wet smear on the ground where she'd landed as she dodged the animal and scraped her palm raw.

Hizzoner lunged. Aimee kicked her boot heel into the dog's muzzle, feeling a crunch in it and a white-hot blast of pain in her ankle.

"Aimee! I'm almost done, but you have to get him back in the center or it won't work!" Stasia shouted.

The black dog's lips peeled away from scarlet gums, and thick ropes of drool spilled to the road. Just when Aimee sensed he would lunge again, the car horn cut loose, warbling shrilly into the darkness and momentarily distracting the black dog. Aimee scrambled to her feet, crouching to make herself a smaller target, and the dog swung back to her again, growling.

Stasia bolted across the intersection right behind the dog. Hizzoner failed to notice her, just as he'd failed to notice when she called out a moment earlier. Stasia held one last wet bundle in her hands as she ran to the side of the road.

Aimee sprinted to the center of the crossroads, where the yellow lines intersected. The dog snarled, muzzle shuddering, and started after her. Aimee cringed, knowing this time he wouldn't miss. But if she blew their only chance, the hellhound would get her father, probably her brother, and maybe her best friend as well. She whimpered as the monster bulleted in her direction. Shane blared the horn again, yelling out the window at the top of his lungs, desperate to get the animal's attention away from her.

Then everything seemed to freeze. The wind stopped moaning; the car horn faded to the dullest whisper. The air itself seemed to congeal around her, and the massive brute hung suspended in the air, teeth bared, eyes narrowed but burning no less fiercely, and a string of saliva hanging like an icicle from its black, gaping maw.

Aimee looked on, amazed, as the wind kicked up, whipping her hair around her face, and tore the black dog apart. Hizzoner hung suspended in the air, rapidly dissipating like smoke in a hurricane. She watched, eyes wide, until the last flecks of the animal were gone.

The world rushed back in: the sounds of the car, of Shane calling to her, of Stasia's feet moving across the ground. Aimee let herself fall to her knees and stared at the place where the black dog had been. She wanted to speak, wanted to tell them that she was okay, but the other sound distracted her too much. Long after his form was gone, Hizzoner's pain-drenched howl continued on, echoing across Sleepy Hollow.

Alan Lancaster was still unconscious when the ambulance came to pick him up, but he was coming around by the time the whole group arrived at the hospital. Now all they could do was wait.

Stasia sat on an uncomfortable chair in the emergency room's waiting area, watching Shane and Aimee pace back and forth in front of her. Her eyes flicked from one to the other. They'd already told each other everything they'd learned while they'd been apart, including Stasia's theory about why the Horseman had targeted them. Shane was even less willing to accept the possibility than Aimee had been. It was just too much—there was no way it was true.

All of them had agreed that they couldn't wait until morning to make their next move. The Horseman was getting ambitious and he might come for Stasia or her father at any time. They had to stop him. The best they could think of was to start by searching the oldest crypts in the Old Dutch Cemetery, which was almost big enough to hide a small army.

Stasia's father was on his way to the hospital, and so were the police. They knew they shouldn't stay, but they also knew they didn't want to leave until Shane and Aimee's father was awake.

"We need to go now, guys." Stasia finally spoke up, tired of listening to the silence between the siblings. The tension was heavy enough that it seemed to pour out of them and crash into the air.

"Where are we going to go, Stasia?" Shane asked. "We can't just leave."

Aimee jumped on that one. "We've got to find the Horseman's head, Shane. We have to stop him before he hurts anyone else." Her eyes locked on his, and she scowled. "You blew it with Dad, but maybe we can still help Stasia and her father."

"I blew it? *I* blew it? If he wasn't always worried about you getting into trouble, he could've trusted you to sleep over at Stasia's and actually stay inside, actually do what he asked. Then we wouldn't have had to drive over there in the first place and none of this would have—"

"You know what I was doing!" she snapped. "I was finding out about the Horseman!" She glared at her brother and he shot her a furious look of his own.

"And what are your excuses for every other day since we got to town? You might not have been doing something stupid tonight, Aimee, but most of the time you are."

"What would you know about it?"

"I'm the one who has to cover for you. I'm the one who gets stuck backing up your lies and making sure Dad doesn't go off the damn deep end trying to figure out where you are when you aren't where you said you'd be." Shane moved toward his sister in a slightly menacing way, like he was about to hit her, and Stasia sat up straighter. The worst part was, she could tell that both of them were actually holding back, not cutting loose with both cannons, because she was there.

Instead of swinging, Shane poked a finger in his sister's face. "I'm the one who has to keep a can of Lysol in his room just in case you come home so wasted that you puke all over the place again. Remember that time in Boston, Aimee? It was me who got stuck cleaning up the bathroom when you missed your little prayer service to the porcelain god."

"I didn't ask you to!"

"I didn't do it for you! I did it for Dad!"

Stasia stood and grabbed each of them by the arm. She looked to Shane first and then to Aimee. "We have to go now. The police will be here any minute, your dad is in safe hands, and my dad is out on the road, driving here to find me and maybe getting a headless freak after his butt. So we have to leave. If you don't come with me, I'll go alone."

A few minutes later they were sliding out the side door of the hospital, Shane and Aimee wearing matching guilty expressions. Stasia knew they wanted to stay with their father. But the Horseman was still out there, and Stasia couldn't stop him alone.

Stasia took the lead and the Lancasters followed. That didn't happen often, though Stasia suspected Aimee would have thought differently and knew Shane would have. Aimee seemed to look at her like a big sister, which was cool, but she didn't seem to notice that most of the time it was Aimee calling the shots and Stasia just enjoying the ride. And Shane? Well, she could see by the way he looked at her sometimes that he thought she was trouble—too intense, too reckless.

That was kind of a shame, really, because he was sweet and smart and funny and there was something between them. Stasia felt it all the time. Of course, it would have been a little complicated with Aimee in the mix anyway. But it was still a shame. She wanted to be his friend at the very least, but Shane pretty much avoided even looking at her or speaking to her when Aimee wasn't around.

Stasia tuned the siblings out as they continued to argue, running over their plan in her head. They would need to check a listing of all of the local cemeteries to see if any others had graves that went back as far as "The Legend of Sleepy Hollow." And they would need tools, but she wasn't exactly sure what kind.

She was new at robbing graves. They'd just have to wing it.

CHAPTER
FIFTEEN

THE OLD DUTCH Settlers Cemetery wasn't what Shane expected. He'd been thinking there might be a hundred or so headstones behind the ancient church. He hadn't expected a forest of statues and memorials to the dead, each more elaborate than the one before. The narrow, rutted paths that had been carved into the ground by cars over the years wound through twenty or more acres of monuments and headstones, with a scattering of trees that ran across the hills rising gently behind the church. He'd seen the spot dozens of times but always from the road, where it was mostly hidden from view.

It was beautiful, creepy, and obscured by endless patches of darkness that could easily hide a horse and rider. The only bonus was that there were low barriers of chains and posts that separated most of the family plots; they might slow the Horseman down. Then again, they might make Shane or the girls fall on their faces if they misjudged while running.

The night wasn't getting any younger. That had always

been one of his mother's favorite sayings, and Shane felt he could understand it for the first time. They were out long after curfew, sneaking around a cemetery just asking to be arrested as vandals. Down the road a siren cut loose, screaming in the distance and coming their way. All three of them ducked down behind headstones and faced the road, hoping not to be spotted by any police. Not long after that they saw the squad car go ripping down the road below, heading toward the center of town again.

Aimee squatted next to Shane, and he could feel her eyes on him. She was glaring, he could tell that too. It was the only expression she seemed to have for him tonight.

As soon as the sirens faded away, she started in again, her voice like a buzz saw on his nerves. "Where do you get off blaming me for Dad being in the hospital? If it hadn't been for Stasia and me doing those wards she came up with, both of you would be dead."

He closed his eyes and counted to ten. "Let's just find the crypt, okay? Then you can whine all you want." He clicked his flashlight back on and started reading engravings on crypts. Van Buren, Keller, Mattias, a whole slew of names, most of them faded in antiquity. Shane and the girls had already gotten into several of the crypts without breaking anything and a handful of others by just forcing the seal with a crowbar. Two they had decided to come back to later if necessary because getting in would require doing some serious damage, which seemed vaguely blasphemous.

They certainly hadn't found a crypt with CRANE inscribed over the door. Aimee had said something about Ichabod Crane changing his name, or had it been in the books he'd looked over earlier? It was all blurring together in his head.

"Fine." Aimee stood and moved away, her body tense with suppressed anger. She looked back over her shoulder at him, eyes narrowed, and said something under her breath.

"Hey, you have something to say, at least say it loud enough to hear, okay?" He'd had it. She'd been bearing down on him all night.

"I said I hope you can remember to cry a little if anyone else dies!"

"What?" He stared hard at his sister, watching her blink rapidly, knowing she was fighting back tears. "Where is that coming from?"

"You know where it's coming from! You're a cold fish, Shane. I always just thought it was lack of personality, but you're cold."

"Jesus, Aimee! Are you starting on Mom again?" His head was pounding, and she was harping on something she didn't understand.

"So what if I am? What if I'm using the best example I ever saw to make my point? Too bad, Shane. The truth hurts."

Shane shook his head. He'd heard this rant one too many times, and he was sick of just letting it go. Sick of

Aimee acting like she'd cornered the market on pain just because he'd kept his inside. "You're *wrong*, Aimee. I cried when Mom died. I just didn't do it around you." He said the words softly. "I spent my whole life coming in second place to the princess, sharing everything with you, and I wasn't going to share my pain with you too. You didn't deserve it. 'Cause what did you give Mom in return? You stole a goddamn car. Never mind coming home drunk."

Aimee reeled back as if she'd been slapped. She looked away from him for a few seconds. "I think we better split up. This will go faster if we take different parts of the graveyard." She walked away before Shane could do much more than blink. "Besides, this way I won't have to hit you with my shovel."

Shane resisted the urge to chase her. He knew he should, but he was so angry that he couldn't help being relieved to have some space. And if she needed him, all she had to do was yell.

Aimee didn't know what he had promised their mom when she was on her deathbed. Dad had been a wreck, though he tried to hide it, and Aimee had been in tears almost constantly when she wasn't throwing tantrums. So he'd promised that he would be strong for them. He hadn't let it show how much her dying by inches tore him up. He hadn't thrown any fits or screamed or cried because, damn it, someone had to be the strong one, and that had been him.

Aimee didn't know any of that, and it wasn't her

business. The more he thought about it, the angrier he got. Damn her for her holier-than-thou outlook, as if his not wanting to show weakness to her and Dad somehow made him less of a human being, less real. She was the one who kept stealing away in the middle of the night, who kept doing every self-destructive little thing she could think of, like sneaking out past their father was the best little rush she could hope for.

His knuckles hurt from squeezing his fists tightly, and most of the muscles in his neck and shoulders throbbed, demanding that he ease up. Shane didn't want to listen. He reveled in his anger because, when you got right down to it, anger was better than feeling nothing at all or even just feeling the pit where his love for his mother had gone. He liked being angry and he liked holding it in. His rage was a private thing that his sister couldn't hope to understand.

He was just really getting into a proper cold fury when he felt the hand on his shoulder, soft, tentative, and warm in the cold night. Shane looked up at Stasia and felt his anger subside.

"Shane, don't be too angry with her. She doesn't mean to take it out on you, you know; it's just that you're all she has. You're the only one she *can* take it out on."

He looked away, uncomfortable with the knowledge that she was so perceptive. "I'm tired of being her whipping boy, Stasia. I have enough problems of my own without her throwing more at me."

The hand on his shoulder squeezed softly and Stasia

stepped in front of him, her fingers leaving trails of warmth where they made contact. "She isn't like you, Shane. She needs to have a sounding board. You can hold it all inside, but Aimee doesn't know how to keep it from coming out. You . . ." She looked into his eyes and he wanted to look away, to avoid her focus, but it was almost impossible. "You're a loner. Aimee is a social creature, and right now the only people she knows are your dad and us. And I'm a friend, Shane, I'm not family."

"That doesn't mean I want to be the one she blames for everything that goes wrong. She's acting like I called Hizzoner out of the woods and begged him to attack the car."

"She knows that's not true." Stasia shook her head, her eyes never leaving his. "But both of you are so busy worrying about your dad that you have to blame someone for everything that happens."

He stared back at her, biting his lip.

"You're worried about her partying getting to your dad," Stasia continued, "and she's worried that your being alone all the time is worrying your dad. You're probably both right, but both of you are acting like he's made of glass, and he isn't. You and your sister lost your mom and that sucks, but you're both okay, and your dad lost his wife and that sucks, but he's going to be okay too."

Stasia gazed into his eyes and Shane felt himself falling, just falling, wanting to hold her. He forced himself to look away.

"I guess so, but I can't get caught up in all that. We can't afford it right now. Let's just find the Horseman's skull, okay?"

"We will, Shane. But I want you to know something."

He looked back at Stasia, ready to hear her defend Aimee some more because really, that's what best friends were supposed to do. Instead she touched his face with her long, delicate fingers and looked him in the eye, her hand stopping him from looking away again. "I care about Aimee. I wouldn't want to do anything to screw up our friendship. But I care about you too. I like you a lot, Shane. I just wanted you to know that."

He swallowed, the words refusing to come out of his mouth. This wasn't the way it was supposed to happen. He stayed on the sidelines and thought about her all the time. But he had never imagined she might feel the same way. He thought about telling her as much and knew he would never get the words out.

Stasia didn't give him the chance. She leaned in and placed her soft, perfect lips against his, urging him to kiss back with a gentle nudge. His heart pounded, his whole universe seeming in that one moment to focus solely on the girl in front of him, on the feel of her lips against his, the feel of her breath touching his face, her hand on his neck. His hands betrayed him and moved to her waist, then lower, holding her close as he tried to absorb every detail of the moment.

And as he savored her kiss, her breath, the feel of

her hips beneath his hands, the slow lingering explosion of all his senses, a scream tore through the night. Shane was ripped back into the nightmare his life had become. He recognized that voice.

"Aimee!"

Aimee tried to calm down. She knew she wasn't being fair to Shane, but she didn't care. Her mother was dead and she had just come too damn close to losing her father too. She needed someone to blame and he was convenient.

Under other circumstances, she'd have been terrified to walk through the old cemetery by herself in the dark. At the moment she was still too pissed to be frightened. The flashlight's beam cut through the darkness well enough for her to see the headstones, and she used it, carefully reading each name as she went. They were looking for a crypt, but she thought it would be smart to check the plain old graves as well, just in case they found a Crane. There were more names in the massive sprawling cemetery than she would have imagined; over three hundred years of history decorated the land here, with bodies that dated back to before the Revolutionary War.

When she came to one of the older crypts and flashed the light across it, it took a moment for what she saw engraved there to register. Then her eyes grew wide and her mouth hung open in surprise. The stone was old and bleak and stained by mold to a sinister shade that was almost black. Weeds licked along the edges, bolder and thicker than they were at most of the other structures within the necropolis. A single name adorned the stonework above the old iron gate that barred easy entrance to the public. It was what she had been searching for, but she realized now that in her heart she had never expected to actually find it.

Crane.

Ichabod himself wouldn't be buried here. That was obvious. It must be a family crypt. But what better place for him to hide Van Tassel's head? The surviving town council members back in those days might have figured out they ought to look here for it, but from what Theodore Hasselbeck's ghost had said, they didn't even know the mayor and the Horseman were one and the same until they'd made their deal with the Horseman and banished Crane from Sleepy Hollow.

Aimee looked at the closed iron doors and pushed tentatively with her foot. There had been a chain on the doors once, but somewhere along the way the thing had fallen into ruin. Though the metal protested and the hinges fairly screamed, the doors pushed inward at her urging.

The night outside was chillingly damp but nothing compared to the atmosphere inside the crypt. Several large stone memorials lay in a neat row along the cobblestone floor of the tomb, and she looked at each of them, reading names. Malachi Crane, Elsbeth Crane,

Walter Crane, Rebekkah Hastings Crane, Matthew Hastings, Roger Hastings, Mary Hastings . . .

There were more Hastings in the Crane family crypt than there were Cranes.

Oh God, she thought, staggering back a step, her flashlight beam wavering as the truth seared across her mind like a falling star streaking across the night sky. Stasia had been right all along. "Oh, no," she whispered.

Hastings.

The words of the ghost of Theodore Hasselbeck rushed into her mind.

Crane lost himself in other places. I have heard whispers of him in the afterlife. When he left Sleepy Hollow, he took another name to hide behind.

Her mother had always said she had family way back when from Sleepy Hollow. It was the thing that had sealed the deal for her father when he had found the job listing for the editor position at the *Gazette.* Small, quiet town, he'd wanted that for them. But he had also liked the idea that they had ancestors here, that in some way his children would be coming home.

Isabel Lancaster's maiden name had been Hastings.

Stasia was right. We're descended right from him, right from the black magic son of a bitch who brought hordes of demons and monsters down on this town. Coming back here, that first night—she had pictures in her mind of the streetlights popping, could still hear the dogs howling and see the windshield splintering—*we brought the curse back with us. The town council vowed to keep us out, and they didn't do that. They're all dead and the vow's probably long forgotten.*

Me and Shane, Aimee thought. *The Horseman's probably saving us for last.*

The Headless Horseman had vowed to rescind his protection and unleash all that he had prevented from running wild in Sleepy Hollow if ever Ichabod Crane or his blood came into Sleepy Hollow again.

"Oh crap, oh crap, oh crap. Oh damn, Shane, we're screwed...."

She grabbed her flashlight and started looking at the different tombs again, wondering which of them held the mayor's skull. She felt sure Crane had hidden it here. Her heart beat double time in her chest and her throat felt dry. It was all their fault! If they hadn't come back to Sleepy Hollow, none of this would have happened.

Crane. I'm descended from Ichabod Crane. The thought made her skin crawl.

Worry about that later. Find the head first. There were several stone coffins in the crypt, both embedded in the walls and placed around the ground, and she knew that in the coffins she would find the remains of the members of that family, laid out on shelves behind the granite plaques engraved with their names. She scurried from plaque to plaque, looking for the name that would make the most sense, wishing she knew more of Ichabod Crane's background so she could make an educated guess. Her heart seemed to take on another beat as she looked, a weird rhythm, and it took her a moment to realize that what she was hearing wasn't a sudden erratic heartbeat.

It was hoofbeats.

From outside the crypt, amid the growing roar of the wind, she heard a neighing sound and cringed. Aimee turned off the flashlight and slipped closer to the opened doors. She peeked through the cleft where the doors were parted and saw a massive black stallion and a man dismounting from the horse. The Headless Horseman.

Aimee grabbed the doors and pushed them toward each other, heart hammering against her rib cage. The Horseman drew his saber and it gave a metallic sigh as it cleared its scabbard. He rushed at the crypt just as the doors clanged shut and she braced herself against them, her skin clammy despite the chill.

The Headless Horseman pushed against the doors and Aimee felt her feet slide across the cobblestones. The doors were thrown open and she fell back, looking up at the hideous demon that had tried to kill her twice already, at that raw, bloody stump where his head had once been.

The demon stalked in her direction, saber raised high. Aimee screamed.

Shane and Stasia ran toward the sound of Aimee's screams, and Shane cursed himself for letting his anger at Aimee override his common sense. Letting her go walking around the cemetery alone had been stupid.

Even worse, he'd let himself get . . . distracted. His lips still burned with the feel of Stasia's kiss, but the rest of him felt frozen. Dread crawled through him like ice forming across the surface of a lake.

Headstones and statuary blurred past as he ran. Stasia tripped when she tried to jump a small dividing line between two plots of land and she sprawled onto the ground. Shane paused, looking back at her in a frenzy of panic.

"Go on!" she said. "Find her. I'm right behind you."

And she was already getting up. Shane took off again, running. Where was Aimee? Then he saw the horse standing near an open crypt.

"Aimee!" He ran harder, moving around the horse, which looked at him with a baleful eye. The horse stomped one foot but otherwise made no move. That was good, really, because the damn thing was scaring the hell out of him.

He pushed into the crypt. The flashlight in his hand cut a swath through the deep shadows in the house of the dead and he saw the Horseman headed for Aimee.

"Get away from her!" Shane screamed, and he ran at the thing, his pulse pounding as adrenaline kicked his system into overdrive. The Horseman turned abruptly and backhanded him across the face, sending him staggering. Shane spilled backward over one of the stone coffins in the center of the vault, flailed his arms as he fell, and struck his head on the cobblestone floor.

With a grunt he sat up. His head rang with the impact and he felt his face already swelling. He peered through the darkness. The Horseman seemed to have a strange kind of luminescence all his own, like those fish who lived in the sunless depths of the ocean and had to develop their own kind of glow. In that glow Shane saw the demon grab Aimee by the throat and lift her from the ground.

Aimee choked, her air supply cut off by the powerful fingers around her neck. Her feet kicked the air and her hands reached up, gripping the Horseman's wrist, desperate to relieve the pressure on her throat.

With that one powerful hand, the Horseman carried her farther into the crypt and pushed her up against the rough brick wall. Her hair caught in the textured clay and pulled free of her scalp in a dozen small places.

Through a field of black flowers that blossomed at the back of her eyes, Aimee saw Shane getting back up again. Her brother's head turned as he looked for something, a weapon of his own, perhaps. She wanted to call out to him but couldn't. There was no breath to draw, no blood flowing to her brain. She felt the darkness closing off her thoughts. The Horseman drew back his saber.

With every ounce of strength left in her, Aimee braced her right foot on the wall behind her and kicked up her left leg, trying the only thing she could think of to keep that sword away from her. Her back scraped cold stone and muscles strained as she kicked the Horseman's sword arm hard enough that he dropped his saber. The blade seemed to moan with disappointment as it struck the ground point first and stood up, vibrating.

She prayed that Shane would be quick enough to take advantage of the moments she'd bought.

But it wasn't Shane who darted through the darkness to reach for the sword. Stasia went for the blade. The Horseman moved to stop her, hauling Aimee away from the wall in the process. Aimee felt a merciful breath of air slide into her and sucked it in deeply as her fingers continued to claw at his gloved hand.

The Horseman reached his weapon first. He hefted the sword and sliced the air inches from Stasia's face. She cried out in fright, stumbling away. She didn't have time to recover before the Horseman shoved Aimee at her, tossing her as though she weighed nothing. Stasia was quicker than Aimee would have guessed. She sidestepped and Aimee sailed right past her. She struck the wall of the crypt and felt her left arm give way with a crack of bone, felt a hundred tiny aches flare up into constellations of agony as her forearm twisted under the impact.

Aimee hit the ground in a pile and stayed there as the Horseman once again moved in her direction. She dragged in breath after breath, feeling blood flow back into her head.

Something gleamed in the shadows. For half a second she thought the Horseman had replaced his head with a shovel blade. Then she saw the shovel swing, cutting through the shadows and striking the Horseman's right shoulder. He was caught off guard and staggered a moment. Which was when Aimee saw that it was Shane wielding the shovel.

Her brother kept swinging, bringing the shovel down hard three times, then a fourth and fifth, staggering the demon a couple of times. Stasia was throwing things at the walking nightmare, her face drawn and her teeth bared. "Come on! You got the wrong girl! I'm over here!"

The Horseman wasn't staggered for long. In silent fury the headless monstrosity swung his sword, the saber merely a blur in the darkness, and cleaved the shovel handle in two. While Shane was still staring wide-eyed, the Horseman cuffed him across the chin with the pommel of his weapon. Her brother stumbled backward and the Horseman advanced on him.

Stasia screamed Shane's name. Then she did the most courageous thing Aimee had ever seen. She rushed the Horseman from behind and grabbed his sword arm, trying to keep the blade from falling.

"Aren't you supposed to kill me first?" Stasia yelled. "Me and my dad? Why don't you pick on me, you freak!"

The Horseman shook her off and Stasia landed across one of the stone coffins, the corner catching her in the stomach so that she grunted with the impact.

Aimee watched it all, her broken arm throbbing savagely. Shane came at the horseman again, swinging the broken shovel handle like a baseball bat and dodging back as the sword flashed at him. Stasia got back up, gasping, holding her stomach and moving toward the Horseman again, and Aimee realized through her pain that they were keeping the Horseman from her. Her brother and her best friend were risking themselves again and again while she tried to recover.

It hurt her more than she thought possible to move, to make her arm take any more pain, but she found the other half of Shane's shovel and gripped it close to the blade. She scooted across the crypt floor to the first of the tombs in the wall and pushed the metal blade against the seam of the plaque that covered the shelf inside. She used her body, throwing her weight on the broken shovel handle again and again, feeling her splintered arm scream with every thrust. Then the granite slab hiding the tomb of Roger Hastings snapped in half, stone thudding to the floor. Aimee dropped the shovel and nearly threw up as she forced herself to work her uninjured arm into the tomb. She felt around inside, encountering bones and cloth and dust. She gagged but made herself keep searching until she was sure there was only one human skull inside.

Shane lowered his head, charging the Horseman. Aimee saw that Stasia had managed to grab the demon's sword hand and was holding on for dear life. Shane hit the Horseman in the stomach with his shoulder and lifted him off the ground for a moment, his arms around the creature's waist. The momentum carried the three of them half a dozen feet and they crashed out the door of the crypt and into the night beyond.

Aimee felt the terror surge as images of Shane and Stasia's decapitated corpses, their bloodied heads tumbling to the ground, swam into her mind. She shoved the thoughts away, hot tears slipping down her face as she used her right hand and the weight of her body to pry the granite face off the second tomb. There was little left of Elsbeth Crane inside the dark chamber except dust and a few pieces of metal. Aimee made herself crawl halfway in to make sure there wasn't a skull hiding somewhere in a corner.

Her body was trembling now, and she was coated in sweat and grave dust. The shovel she'd been using had broken further, leaving little more than a blade that wouldn't allow her any real leverage. Outside the tomb the black monster of a horse let out a deep, threatening neigh and Stasia responded with a stream of curses. At least she was still alive.

Rebekkah Hastings Crane gave up her secrets only grudgingly. Aimee's heel was broken and bloody inside her shoe by the time she'd managed to work the shovel into the slit between stones and then kicked the tomb open. Her stomach threatened to expel every meal she'd had since the day she was born and her mouth felt sour with the promise of vomiting, her hands were shaking like leaves in a wind tunnel, and her skin practically glowed white even in the near darkness of the Crane family crypt. Aimee made herself slither into the darkness of the tomb, gasping hard and forcing herself to stay conscious despite the spikes of agony that shot up from her broken bone. Her brother needed her and Stasia needed her and she didn't want to pass out in the remains of some distant ancestor.

Aimee's hands slid along a body that felt far too fresh to be as old as it was supposed to be. She could feel muscle and flesh and clothing. Her fingers touched thick growths of mold and something wet and cold slithered over her hand. Resting on the crossed arms of Rebekkah Hastings Crane, cupped in the corpse's upturned hands like a grisly bouquet of bone, she found a human skull.

Hollow now, nothing but numbness and cold inside, lanced with pain from her broken arm, Aimee grabbed her prize with her good hand and slithered backward out of the dark tomb. Tears flowed from her eyes and her heart beat as fast as a hummingbird's wings. Her arm let out a screaming choir of agonies to dance over her nerve endings and send waves of pain through her entire body.

She staggered and wove through the crypt until she made it to the doors, which seemed like they were a hundred miles away. Her knees shook, her legs nearly refused to do what she told them to, and she clutched the skull through the eye sockets like a bowling ball.

Cool night air felt like an arctic kiss against her

flesh and she looked outside to see the Horseman clap his hand on Shane's forearm as he drew back the saber again, ready to take her brother's head in vengeance for centuries-old betrayal. Stasia was backed against the side of the crypt, the huge black horse pressing her against the stone as if to crush her. Stasia's hands beat uselessly at the animal's skull.

Adrenaline gave Aimee one last brilliant gasp of energy and coherent thought. She looked at the Horseman's back and called out to him.

"Baltus Van Tassel!"

The demon turned sharply, the sword still held high.

"Catch it, you freak!"

She hurled the skull at the Horseman. He caught it easily and held the prize he had sought for over two centuries. The demon shoved Shane away and sheathed his sword. Then, with a clap of his gloved hands, he summoned his steed away from Stasia, who fell to her knees, sobbing for air and trembling violently.

Shane gasped at Aimee in amazement.

The Horseman's cloak rustled in the strong breeze, the promise of the oncoming storm, and then he mounted his horse, still holding the skull in his hand. Holding his own head, taken from him so long ago by Aimee and Shane's ancestor. Heels drove into equine flanks and the stallion reared up high, balancing on its hind legs. The Horseman dropped the skull on the ground and the horse drove its powerful, iron-clad hooves down, shattering the thick bone, grinding it to dust.

Without a backward glance, the Horseman rode hard off through the graveyard and into the woods, swallowed by the darkness.

Aimee managed three steps forward before her legs gave out. Somehow Shane was there to catch her.

EPILOGUE

SHANE HATED HOSPITALS. He'd seen three of his four grandparents last when they were in hospitals. He had watched his mother die by slow degrees in the hospital, trying her best to smile when she was obviously in pain. Toward the end he'd dreaded visiting her. He'd always managed a smile because she needed those in the last days, but it had never been easy.

So he entered the room with a flurry of butterflies trying to rip their way from his stomach and held his breath until he saw that Aimee was okay. He thought she was asleep, but then she opened her eyes and smiled wanly in his direction.

"Hey." Her voice was dry and raspy. "What are you doing here?"

"What do you think I'm doing? I'm checking to see how my sister's holding up."

"Been better, been worse." She held up the cast on her left arm. Shane swallowed the lump of guilt that tried to worm into his throat and strangle him. What had happened probably would have happened anyway, even if he hadn't let Aimee walk off on her own, even if he hadn't been kissing Stasia. Or at least he told himself that, hating that it felt so much like a lie.

They hadn't waited for an ambulance to get Aimee to the hospital. Instead they'd picked her up and helped support her all the way down to the emergency room, where she shared a space with her father for a while before he was released. He'd needed four stitches across his scalp, though Shane would have guessed he'd require a few hundred from the blood that had spilled across the interior of the car.

Shane touched the cast that ran up to just below his sister's elbow and shook his head. "I'm sorry it happened the way it did, Aimee."

Aimee chuckled. "I'm not." She sat up in bed and unconsciously brushed off his effort to help her. "It could have been a lot worse. I swear, you and Stasia both act like it's your fault that a monster came after me."

"I didn't want to see you getting hurt. That's all."

"Well, I didn't want to get hurt either, but it beats the heck out of getting decapitated." She looked at him for a second and frowned. "How's Dad?"

"Pissed off."

"Why? We're okay."

"But we got attacked, you got hurt, and he can't touch the guy that did this to you."

"Yeah, demon from hell and all . . ."

"He still thinks it's a human being, remember?"

"Couldn't prove otherwise to him if we tried."

Shane nodded. The police chief and his dad had been complaining at and to each other about the whole situation when he left this morning. Everyone was looking for a quick solution, and that wasn't going to happen. Shane hadn't heard all of the conversation, but he'd heard enough to know that the current mayor of Sleepy Hollow was being a little bit threatening when it came to Burroughs's continued employment. There was a serial killer on the loose out there and three unsolved murders to go along with him. Shane and Aimee weren't about to tell anyone what they had seen last night in the cemetery. What they had done. No one would have believed them.

"Shane."

He looked at his sister.

"I'm sorry about yesterday. The fighting, I mean."

He felt awkward. This was what he had planned to say to her and she'd put him off balance by bringing it up first. "What's going on with us, Aimee? I mean, we always fought. But we used to be a lot tighter, you know? We used to actually sort of like each other, even during the fighting. But now that seems like all we do."

"I know." She shrugged. "It's just . . . we all deal with stuff our own way. I know Dad gets stressed about me going out and all, but I've got to have a life or I'll go crazy. Then you get all, like, you're the dad, and that pisses me off because he's just as stressed about you."

Shane nodded. "I know. But come on, you *do* go out too much. I've seen your report cards. You could have straight A's. You used to. But ever since Mom got sick, it's like all you do is try to avoid being around me and Dad."

"That's not true." But he could tell by the tone of her voice she knew it was. "I just get claustrophobic hanging around at home. I know school's important, but it's just not as important to me as it is to you or to Dad. Jesus, Shane, it's like they expect us to give up our lives for this crap."

"That's not it, Aimee. You know it and I know it. You're putting this distance between us. Well, in case you were wondering, it hurts, okay?"

Aimee looked at him for a long, long time before she nodded. Her right hand crept up and touched his fingertips. He captured her own fingers before she could think of pulling back and squeezed softly.

"You do it too," she said.

Shane didn't answer and she continued after a pause.

"I know you aren't always doing homework, okay? You started pushing yourself away from your friends in Boston, and aside from now and then talking to Jekyll and Hyde, you've barely even tried to make any friends here."

"Yeah . . ." He muttered the rest of his thought under his breath.

"Yeah, what?" Aimee pressed.

"I said it beats getting close to anyone. You aren't close to them, they can't hurt you."

"Everyone can hurt you, Shane. It's part of living." Aimee looked out the window, staring at the roof of the next wing on the hospital as if it were the most amazing piece of art she had ever seen. "What was that movie we watched? With Morgan Freeman in prison?"

"The Shawshank Redemption?" They'd seen it together one night toward the end of their mother's suffering. He wondered why she'd bring it up now.

"The main character, that tall guy, he says something to Morgan Freeman at the end. You've got two choices in the world. 'You can get busy living or you can get busy dying.' I got busy living, Shane. I might be hiding away from you and Dad sometimes and I might get myself in trouble from time to time, but I got busy living. I left the dying for Mom."

He could have been angry with her, probably would have been, but as she said the words her face collapsed and her eyes shut tightly. Her breath hitched and she started crying again, shedding tears that he thought were long gone from her.

Shane sat on the bed next to his sister and put an arm around her shoulders. He wasn't like her. That was what he always claimed, but he could understand her. He hid from pain; she ran away from it. In the end, they were both doing their best to dodge the sting of their mother's death, and in the end they were both failing all the time.

Aimee leaned her face against his chest and cried softly. He was a bit surprised when he realized he was crying too, but this time he let it happen.

Two days later they walked to school together, Shane carrying Aimee's books though she claimed she could manage just fine. Halfway there Stasia joined them. The memory of her kiss still lingered in Shane's mind. But he did his best not to think about how Stasia made him feel inside because whenever he felt that flutter in his chest, he couldn't help also shuddering with the memory of Aimee's screams and the dull wet snap of her arm breaking.

Stasia gave him a very small smile, and after that she almost ignored him. He understood and reciprocated.

They drifted through their day, Shane avoiding conversations about their experience as much as possible. Aimee told people she'd been attacked but that the man on the horse had fled when he heard the police. That little story spread fast and far in the school, and others told tales of what they had seen or heard over the weekend. Most had seen nothing more than the many police cars that cruised the late-night town roads. The curfew was still in effect, of course, since the murders weren't yet solved.

At lunch the three of them talked as they always

did, and if Stasia was as uncomfortable around Shane as he was around her, Aimee didn't seem to notice.

"Okay, let me get this straight." Shane couldn't quite keep the edge out of his voice. "Old Ichabod couldn't do anything right. If he'd done the ritual correctly in the first place, sacrificed his own life, the Horseman would have been protecting the town all this time. But he cheated when he used Van Tassel's death instead of his own for the ritual. The old town council made their deal to try to get the Horseman under control."

Stasia had that little eager smile of hers back, playing around the corners of her mouth. Now that everyone she cared about was safe, she was thrilled all over again that this stuff was real. "Right. But the deal was he'd stay away and keep the old-school creeps away as long as none of Crane's descendants came back, and like Aimee already figured out . . ."

Aimee nodded. "Us coming back blew the deal." She paused. "Hasselbeck's ghost was right about the head. The Horseman wanted it. And maybe it wasn't just that. Maybe we disrupted the original ritual by taking it out of that crypt. The thing is, we bought our own lives by giving him his head back. But the other stuff . . ."

Stasia focused on Shane. "Look at it this way. Once upon a time all this stuff existed in the world. In the last two hundred years or so all the goblins and demons and everything died or ended up in someplace of their own. But the Horseman had captured all the things that

Crane drew here with his half-assed magic. When the bargain was broken by you guys coming back, the Horseman set them all free. Now, even if he's satisfied to have his head back and isn't going to kill anyone else, that doesn't mean he's going to round up the nasties again."

"But it doesn't mean he won't," Aimee added. "We don't know."

"I'm betting we'll know soon enough," Stasia said.

"Okay," Shane said. "I get it. But we didn't undo the ritual completely, because he's still out there. Only with no bargains in place and no rituals to control him, he's completely free to do whatever he wants. What I want to know is, what's he going to do now that he's free?"

None of them had an answer for that.

"Well, Amber Dunfee did tell me today that she saw the Horseman at sunset last night," Aimee spoke up. "That he rode hard down her street and up into the hills above Sleepy Hollow. I thought—I thought maybe she had the day wrong, but I don't know. . . ."

The three exchanged nervous glances. "I guess we just wait and see," Aimee said quietly. They ate in silence for a minute, and then Stasia and Aimee started a new conversation, something about one of the cheerleaders.

Shane let his attention drift, gazing out the window. Autumn was in full swing now and the foliage was a burst of colors, leaves turning red, orange, and gold.

Several trees' branches were already nearly bare. A fat squirrel sat on a limb and gnawed at an acorn. Shane watched it without really seeing until a darkness caught his eye. On the same branch, closer to the center of the tree, something moved with predatory grace, almost like a cat. But cats didn't have wings. Beside him Aimee reached over and thumped him with her cast. She had noticed it too and wanted to make sure he was paying attention. He was.

They both saw the dark, winged thing explode across the tree in a wild blur of speed and snatch the squirrel in its mouth, blood flying from the spot where the squirrel had been perched a second earlier.

The siblings stared, stunned by the sudden violence.

A moment later Stasia cleared her throat. "When I said we'd know soon enough, I wasn't, like, inviting a demonstration. But I guess it's pretty clear that the nasties are still on the loose. The Horseman isn't doing us any favors."

"No, but why should he?" Shane asked, looking at the tree as if it could somehow answer. "Ichabod Crane caused all of this. What now, you know? I mean, there's got to be someone out there to take care of this stuff, someone who knows how to handle these things."

"Yeah, there was. He was trying to kill us a couple of nights ago." Stasia stared out the window for a second longer and then gathered up her backpack as the warning bell rang, sounding more like a scream.

Aimee sighed. "Which just leaves us."

Shane raised an eyebrow. "Us?"

"Our ancestor made this mess. Without knowing it, we stirred it up again. And we're the only ones who know the whole story. Can you think of anyone else?"

Shane felt cold inside. "I wish I could."

ACKNOWLEDGEMENTS

The authors would like to thank Liesa Abrams and Eloise Flood at Razorbill, who worked tirelessly to make sure *The Hollow* came alive; Jim and Bonnie Moore, without whom the series would not exist; and Peter Donaldson, Harris Miller, Jay Sanders, Brant Rose, David Simkins, Jane Leisner, Ross Richie, and Andrew Cosby, for their faith and input.

Chris would like to thank Connie and the kids, as well as Tom Sniegoski, Lisa Clancy, Amber Benson, Jose Nieto, Bob Tomko, Ashleigh Bergh, and Allie Costa for their constant support. Also, a shout out to Liesalicious!

Ford would like to thank Chris for being such a great collaborator and an ideal creative partner; Tomm Coker, Susana Santiago, Jeff Parker, John Byers, and Kyle Carpenter for their support, inspiration, and being good sounding boards; and Washington Irving for the inspiration.